THE TWINKLE IN HER EYE

DAVID A. DIPESA

DORRANCE PUBLISHING CO
EST. 1920
PITTSBURGH, PENNSYLVANIA 15238

Dorrance Publishing Co
585 Alpha Drive
Suite 103
Pittsburgh, PA 15238
Visit our website at www.dorrancebookstore.com

ISBN: 979-8-8881-2008-8
eISBN: 979-8-8881-2508-3

This book is for all of those people who ever believed in me. I cannot begin to express my deepest gratitude and appreciation for all you've meant in my life. I've written stories for many years but I never expected to be here, today, witnessing the advent of my first book. I love writing, more than anything, and I can only hope that my stories will evoke powerful emotions from my audience.

I wish to thank anyone who's read my work in the past and any of those who will in the future. This book was written during an extremely dark period of my life where I can only describe the feeling of being utterly lost as my day-to-day normal. Those days seem so distant now but after going through multiple page proofs of this novel, I feel like I relive them more than I ever wanted to.

Anyway, it's with great pride that I dedicate these pages to the ones who helped me find myself again. I owe those who stood by me more than I can ever repay. I urge anyone who's reading this book to reach out to family or friends that are deeply in pain and let them know that you care. It's never too late!

"If you walk in front of me, I'll never catch up to you.

If you walk behind me, I'll never see you.

But if you walk beside me, I'll never feel alone again."

SHE WAS BREATHTAKING. Her silky auburn hair lightly swept across her bare shoulders. A pallid complexion only accentuated perfect features unable to be captured on camera. When she laughed, it was like a flock of meadow larks singing in the spring. Her heel-toe walk was as silent as a cat stalking prey. Cupid's *bow* lips, elegantly shaped and inviting, emerald eyes and a lithe body that curved in all the right places… she was perfect in every sense of the word. However, nothing was more striking than that speckle of stardust in her right eye. The milky white of her sclera reached out to the verdant splendor of her iris, but it were as though some of the light filtering through gathered in the lower corner of the iris creating a sparkle of gold—a shooting star.

It was impossible not to notice this about Gwendolyn. She couldn't go anywhere without someone commenting on the unusualness of this alien, fantastic feature. They were drawn in, centered on it like moths to flame. That star in her eye… the sun's corona peeking through the lush greenery of a secluded paradise.

Sean watched her intently through his ordinary dark brown eyes. She smiled at him as she brushed a few strands of her bangs away from her forehead.

"I'm *really* glad you asked me out, Sean. I was beginning to think you were some obsessed stalker instead of a true gentleman."

"Oh… I didn't mean to give you that impression. It's just… well, you know."

"Know what?" She furrowed her brow playfully, meadow larks chirping cajolingly.

"Well, I didn't think you were available, for starters. Secondly, just look at the two of us. You're obviously something special, and I'm not."

Gwen suppressed the urge to laugh. This was hardly the confident exchange she'd expected to hear on a first date. Gwen imagined that Sean would be bragging about his yacht or talking about his summer home in Argentina, and how all the women he met begged to be taken there.

"Okay. Why don't we start over? I'm not so full of myself that I would say no to a nice, handsome guy looking to take me out. The proof is right here, isn't it? If I didn't see something I liked then I wouldn't be here." Her cadence was both breathy and stern.

"I just can't help but notice all the men, and even a few women, staring so blatantly at you all evening. I feel like all the attention in this room is on *you*. You're so beautiful… I'm not sure I've *ever* seen a woman as beautiful as you. I just started to feel like maybe I'm a pity date. It's okay if I am. I just wanted to take you out, you know?"

Again, Gwendolyn flashed her inviting smile. She reached her hand across the table and took his, gently massaging his palm with her fingertips. Sean felt his pulse pounding in his ears. She felt so warm.

"I'm going to go to the ladies' room. Why don't you think about a new topic of conversation? When I come back we can move forward as if the last part of this conversation never happened. Okay?"

Sean nodded once. He watched her leave the table, following the curve of her calves to the hem of her strapless black dress that dangled right above her knees. She turned her head once to look back at her date. He looked so smitten. She was pleased.

Gwendolyn returned moments later. She smiled and folded her hands on top of one another—elbows lightly touching against the table.

"Alright. So, what did you come up with?"

"I was just thinking about your right eye. That speckle of gold that almost looks like a beauty mark is very unusual."

Gwen looked away for an instant. She sighed and turned back to Sean, who seemed to be looking more and more like a sad puppy than the confident man that started off the evening.

It always comes back to this.

"Would you tell me how you got it? What's the story behind it?"

"I will make you a promise, Sean. Why don't we get through this evening first? If we decide to have a second date then I'll tell you all about it."

Sean seemed to perk up at those words.

"Sure, Gwendy. I can't wait."

*   *   *

Even with the shades open the sun's rays barely pierced the darkness of the room. It was like a perpetual shadow creature was consuming all the light—appetite never to be sated.

"What's the story here?" a husky man's voice practically echoed through the apartment. He walked tall and poised as he bent low to take a look at the body.

"It looks like a suicide, Detective. 9mm. Guy ate the gun and then, blam! All she wrote."

"How long's he been like this?"

"I'd say given the state of the body and pooling of brain, skull and co-agulated blood that this happened three, maybe four days ago. Although, the smell is a good indicator too."

"Do we have an ID yet?"

"Yeah, it's the guy who lives here, Sean Hammond. He hadn't gone to work for a couple of days so someone came by to check on him. When he didn't answer the door, we got the call."

The detective with the husky voice tossed his coat haphazardly onto the sofa in the living room. He put on a pair of opaque plastic gloves and came back in for a deeper look. He made note of what was left of the expression of the unfortunate Mr. Hammond.

"His eyes are sullen, greatly distressed."

"Well, fuck. The guy blew his brains out. I'd say he was distressed."

"From the positioning of the hands holding the gun and the fetal posi-tion of the body this looks pretty desperate, but you know, something seems off here."

"Besides most of his head?"

"Cute. I'm talking about the man himself as well as the act. Look at this apartment. Look at his clothes and possessions. I'm not convinced he har-bored the kind of desperation involved in doing something like this. Finish up your work here, and get me a report on this as soon as possible. I'm going to interview the neighbors and some people from his office. If this is a homi-cide, and it very well could be, then it's perfectly staged *not* to look like one."

The detective picked up his coat and draped it across his arm. He took one last look around at the former dwellings of Sean Hammond. The apart-ment had the stench of wealth and success and now, sadly, of death.

*   *   *

His smile gleamed brightly. His gaze never faltered. He just couldn't stop looking, even if he wanted to. This man was very handsome. His facial hair was immaculately groomed and his skin was the color of the sand covering the beaches of a tropical island—the kind that tickled your bare feet as you walked across it. Gwendolyn counted out his legal tender and placed it on the counter. She smiled brazenly.

"Will that be all today, sir?"

He hesitated. He just couldn't make himself turn away from her.

"I don't suppose you're free tonight?"

"Free? I happen to be quite expensive, Mr. Saunders."

Gwen laughed along with her customer. Their voices played off one another beautifully.

"Well. I'd imagine a woman as beautiful as you is quite a rare and precious gem."

"Thank you. I think I rather like being compared to a precious gem."

She brushed some of her hair behind a delicate earlobe—face flush and suddenly warm.

"Look, I know I'm just another customer here, but would you have dinner with me tonight?"

Gwen craned her neck to see around her tall gentleman caller. He was holding up quite a long line just to flatter her. She giggled lightly.

"Sure. Would you mind picking me up here at eight?"

"I'd love to."

"Great. Now, you might want to get going. If that line gets any longer you'll be picking me up closer to nine-thirty."

"Oh. Sorry. I just…."

"It's alright. I'm glad you did. See you tonight, Mr. Saunders?"

"Call me Jeffery, please."

Jeffery Saunders lingered a little longer, even as he stepped aside to let the next customer through. He couldn't explain it but his skin was aflame with desire. His very mouth was dry. As Jeffery turned to leave he could've sworn something sparkled brilliantly in the light. It was only about half of a second of a flash but it felt like it came from behind the counter where Gwendolyn worked meticulously.

Her warm, friendly smile greeted all her customers, always. However, as she watched Jeffery exit onto the street, she couldn't help but smile a little wider than usual.

*   *   *

Not a single person said anything disparaging or negative about Sean Hammond. He was a model employee, a respectful tenant and even a social juggernaut who frequented the local clubs and bars often. He built a solid reputation of excellence in the computer software business along with three others. Their clientele ranged from wealthy corporations to small family-owned firms.

Sean worked from 7:00 A.M. to 3:00 P.M. and hit the gym four days a week. When he wasn't at the gym he seemed to have a busy schedule revolving around softball practice and weekend games as well as tennis lessons at a private club in the city, which he had started at the beginning of this year.

Every interview was a carbon copy of the last. He'd had everything going for him.

A call was coming through from the department. The detective answered his phone in his usual low, throaty but direct manner.

"What do you have for me?"

"It was definitely a suicide. Power burns and gun residue are all over our deceased and the exit wound is consistent with our self-inflicted gunshot scenario. The only prints in the entire apartment belong to our guy so nothing there to suggest foul play."

"I see." The detective lingered on the hiss of his last word.

"Sean Hammond took his life. Some people don't need a clear-cut reason to end things, you know?"

"Yeah. His personal effects…. Did you find a cellphone on him when he died?"

"As a matter of fact, we did. It was in the front pocket of his pants. Why?"

"Normally, the truly desperate look for a reason *not* to do it. His phone in such close proximity says that he was waiting for someone to either talk him out of it or possibly ready to place a call for the exact same reason. Did the tox screen reveal anything?"

"He was totally clean. Not even a drop of alcohol in his system."

"Alright, I'm going to stop by and have a look through his cellphone. There might be someone in his contacts that I didn't question yet."

"Detective. I don't mean to overstep here but it seems like you might be reaching. Sean Hammond committed suicide. Forensics has completed their sweep and the evidence is conclusive."

Lawrence felt a migraine coming on. He massaged his left temple and closed his eyes for a brief second.

"Detective?"

"I'm still here. I know what this appears to be, but I want one last go at it before it's buried. If his phone's a dead end then we close it."

Lawrence hung up his phone and proceeded to the street corner where he parked his car. A bright orange parking ticket on his windshield set his blood to boil. He snatched the ticket, crinkled it in his hand and tossed it on the passenger seat.

"Two minutes over…. Fuckin' meter maids. No respect for anyone on the job."

*   *   *

Jeffery's sleek BMW pulled into the parking lot at exactly 7:58 P.M. She was standing on the curbside closest to the building's doors and security cameras. Her short purple mini-skirt was accented by black diamond patterns on the sides. The skirt was above the knee, showing off an incredible set of toned legs. She wore the same floral blouse from earlier but there appeared to be a few buttons from the top undone—the metal strap from her crossbody purse draped over her body like a thin chain snake. She stood with one leg leading and knee slightly bent, a wanton pose meant to capture and captivate. Jeffery cut the engine and leapt out of the car. He was dressed casual, in his expensive charcoal silk shirt and matching dress pants. He took Gwendolyn by the hand and led her to the passenger side, opening the door for the lady. She felt overcome with excitement as she stepped inside, crossing one leg slowly over the other. Her date was fixated on her and she was enjoying every moment of it.

The car sped off. This was already promising to be quite a memorable evening.

*   *   *

The restaurant was like nothing Gwen had ever seen. She remarked that the luxurious chandelier in the grand dining room was at least the size of a small crater in the moon. The lights reflected off crystal adornments, which only made the room seem brighter. Jeffery sat across from her with his dark eyes and charming smile. She felt like a princess.

"So, where are you from, Gwendolyn?"

"So formal. Please, call me Gwendy."

"Alright, Gwendy."

"Well, my father was in the military so I had to spend a lot of time across country and even some overseas. Eventually, *I* settled here."

"So you didn't stay close to family then?"

"No."

"So, why here? What do you like about here?"

"Everything. My life is practical and, at times, can be a bit mundane, but it's exactly what I've always wanted. What about you, Jeffery Saunders? You're not originally from here either, are you?"

"No. My family is from Goa. I have a dominating, lively Portuguese bloodline, hence why I don't look as Indian as most from my country."

Their conversation continued well into the night. Gwendy was enjoying herself, and Jeffery seemed to be pulling deeper into her with each passing moment. He was very charming and humble. She loved that about him.

"So, perhaps you hear this often, but you have fantastic eyes."

"I do, but thank you. I never get tired of compliments." She shied away in a teasing manner.

"Your right eye has this enchanting speckle of gold in it. I've noticed that it flares beautifully in the light. It's so unusual…. It really suits you."

"Glad you like it."

"How is this possible? Is it a birthmark or maybe even a defect of the eye?"

"I'm not really sure. It's always been there."

"I… I, um, just would love to know more about it."

His last comment seemed unsure and lacked the confidence with which his conversation had previously flowed throughout the night. Gwendolyn could hear a hesitation in his voice. He was focusing solely on that twinkle in her right eye.

Jeffery took a large gulp of his drink and continued to stare.

"So… we have just about closed the restaurant." Gwen laughed as she looked around at the lack of customers seated.

"You must have a lot of admirers, Gwendy. I hope you didn't decide to go out with me out of pity. But, even if you did… I sincerely don't mind. Just being in your presence is enough for me."

"I chose to be here with you because I wanted to. I think you're giving me way too much credit. Sure, I have admirers but I don't give in so easily to a wink, nice smile or some flirting."

She extended her hand to his. Jeffery felt his heart race. He took Gwendy's hand graciously. His gaze never left hers. Those eyes…. They were a lush, elegant green with a single shooting star hidden within only one of them. They were perfect. *She* was perfect.

*   *   *

Lawrence scrolled through the log in Sean's cellphone. There was a recurring number, but the calls were never longer than just a few seconds and no text messages either. There was also no name associated with the number in his address book. Judging by the frequency, this contact was relatively new but he'd placed quite a few calls to them. Surely they were good enough to add to his address book. It looked like he'd had started calling this person around six or maybe seven days before his body was discovered. Could this be the lead Lawrence was hoping for? It couldn't hurt to have the number traced. If this person was familiar with Sean Hammond, then maybe they'd know why he decided to kill himself.

*   *   *

Gwen slipped off her shoes and tossed her designer handbag on the couch. Dinner was lovely. She couldn't finish all of her meal, so she'd had it wrapped up in some sort of tinfoil swan/sea monster amalgamation. She put the meal in the fridge and headed for the bedroom. She wore a light smile as she hummed a random pop song she'd heard in the car as she and Jeffery headed back from the restaurant. Gwendolyn suddenly laughed. The song would probably get stuck in her head for the next three days leading her to search for the mp3 online, download it and listen to it for the next six months. Years from now she'd stumble upon the song while grocery shopping and resurrect the old mp3 that she swore she was sick of hearing.

She exited her bedroom clad in a short purple silk robe, pinning her hair up. The sound of her tub filling with water echoed through the hallway adjoining the bedroom to the living room. The girl giddily skipped across the floor to her laptop. With the tub filling up, she had some time to kill. Perhaps she'd look for that song after all.

*   *   *

The unlisted number in Sean's phone came up as a cellphone belonging to a Ms. Gwendolyn M. O'Hara. The girl made a modest living as a bank teller while teaching piano lessons three times a week for some extra cash. She even reported her side income to the IRS. Lawrence scratched his head. He'd expected this number to belong to either a bookie or even a loan shark. Lawrence sat in an uncomfortable chair outside a small office. His back was bothering him so he shifted uneasily in the seat, trying to find the one position that didn't feel like a steel rod was digging into his spinal cord.

The door to the office opened and a well-dressed man with a trendy hairstyle waved for Lawrence to come his way.

"Thank you for taking time out to see me again, Mr. Hoffman. I know you're a busy man."

"Well, anything I can do to help the police explain Sean's death. His family deserves to know the truth, no matter how gruesome it might be. So, there's still an investigation then? I thought this was a suicide."

Lawrence sat across from Mr. Hoffman.

Now this chair is actually comfortable.

"While the evidence is conclusive enough to rule this one a suicide, I'm not convinced. Everything I've learned about Sean Hammond doesn't point to such drastic action."

"Yeah, you and me both. Kid was a dynamo with a hell of a lot going for him."

"Did Sean ever mention a woman by the name of Gwendolyn O'Hara?"

"Did he? Gee, only like every single hour after he met her. I hear his boasting was perfectly justified too. I mean, anyone who's seen this girl says that she's a real dish. The guy who comes for our shred bins also does the ones at the bank where she works. That's how Sean found out about her, and he always said she was the finest piece in the entire city."

"Did the two of them ever meet up? Did they date or have a casual fling?"

"I think so. I mean, after all his incessant bragging, I sure hope he took her out."

"So, he never mentioned their date at all?"

"Come to think of it… no… nothing I can remember."

"I see. Thank you for your time, Mr. Hoffman."

Lawrence rose, shook the man's hand and hurried out the door. A man bigheaded about taking a beautiful woman out on the town wasn't out of the ordinary. However, not saying a word about it usually meant it didn't go so well. Gwendolyn O'Hara wasn't a suspect, but if she'd had a date with Sean then maybe she'd remember if anything seemed off about him that night.

*   *   *

Gwen counted out ten large bills and placed them on the counter.

"Is there anything else I can do for you today, ma'am?" Her smile was infectious.

"No, thank you."

"Then you have a lovely day."

"Thank you, Gwendy. You're always so pleasant."

"Hey, that's why they hired me."

A man approached her window with an arresting presence. Gwen almost shrank back as she made eye contact. His gray eyes could only be described as severe, and the skin around them, weathered. His hair was short-cropped, salt-and-pepper but more pepper than salt. He went for something inside his jacket. The teller looked to the associate next to her and then to the guard at the front of the building. A badge was produced introducing this man as a homicide detective.

"My name is Lawrence Stowell. May I have a word with you, Miss O'Hara?"

"May I ask what this is about?" Gwen looked anxiously to her boss, who was making her way over to her window.

"I want to talk to you about Sean Hammond."

"Is everything okay here, Gwendy?"

"Yes, ma'am. This is Detective Stowell. He has some questions about a man I met here at the bank. May I take an early lunch?"

"Sure. Take as much time as you need."

"I don't think I'll be a full hour, but on the off chance that I am, I'll make up the time."

Her boss placed a hand on her shoulder, eyeing Lawrence as if he were a Gestapo officer. "It's alright. I can cover your regulars."

Gwendolyn grabbed her spring beige coat and headed out the front door with the detective in tow. Lawrence couldn't help but comment to himself that Gwendolyn's reputation was well deserved. Not only was she beautiful but she seemed as sweet as melted marshmallow over chocolate.

*   *   *

"Did you and Sean Hammond ever meet up, Miss O'Hara?"

"Yes, I saw him. He took me out on a date about two weeks ago. He was a perfect gentleman, albeit somewhat nervous and unsure of himself, but still, a perfect gentleman." Gwen raised her coffee cup to her delicate, full lips and took a gentle sip. There was no noise save for a tiny sigh that spoke of pure satisfaction. Her eyes smiled along with her mouth as she looked up at Lawrence.

"Unsure of himself and nervous aren't exactly painting the picture of the Sean Hammond that I've pieced together, Gwendolyn. It seems that you're the only one who saw him this way."

"What is this about, Detective? We had only one date and then I never heard from him again. And I was really looking forward to a second date too. I liked him. He was sincere and really cute."

"Then you don't know?" Lawrence raised an eyebrow as he took a drink of his beverage.

"Know what?"

"Sean was found dead in his apartment a couple of days ago. They're calling it a suicide."

Gwendolyn almost dropped her cup.

"Oh, my…. He killed himself? But… why? How?"

"If you really want to know he used a 9mm. I think you can fill in the blanks to this Mad Lib. I went through his phone and found an excessive amount of calls placed to your cell number. The call durations were only five seconds at longest, three seconds minimum, and the frequencies were about ten times every day until about maybe a day or two before his death."

"I… I remember getting some strange hang-up calls, but then they stopped all of sudden. I was about to change my number out of agitation."

"Did he ever reach out? Did he ever engage you in conversation at all, or try?"

"No. If it was him, he never uttered a word. I gave him my number the night we went out, but when I didn't hear from him, I figured maybe he met someone else or just wasn't interested anymore."

"I'm sorry I have to ask, but did you and he…."

"No. I do *not* make a habit of sleeping with someone on a first date. He was a customer at the bank and that's how I met him. I had him pick me up as well as drop me off here. We didn't even kiss. I lingered a little longer in the passenger seat, but he never even made a move. Anyway, the bank security cameras can corroborate my story."

"I'm sorry I had to ask about any intimacy. I'm just looking for anything to explain the circumstances surrounding his death so that his family can have some closure."

Gwen reached out and took both of Lawrence's hands in her own. Her fingertips massaged his palms almost lovingly.

"I've learned that life can be messy. I've moved around a lot, and I've seen firsthand that sometimes the simplest of explanations are usually the correct ones. I know it's tragic, but maybe Sean Hammond really did take his own life because he was unhappy. Maybe that unhappiness was buried so deeply inside him that it started to eat its way out, and Sean couldn't deal with the pain anymore. He was such a nice guy and his family can have that to hold on to, Detective. If you'd like, I can call them and let them know what a true gentleman they raised. I would only be stating a fact and I'd be honored to do it."

"There's no need for that, Gwendolyn."

Lawrence looked deeply into the teller's eyes. That sparkle. That singular supernova inside her right eye caught his attention. It was so mysterious and unique.

"What is it?" Gwen looked around.

"Your eye. I imagine you get a lot of questions about that speckle of gold in it."

"Oh, that." She placed a hand over the eye and flushed a shade of the prettiest pink.

"It's very unique. Would you mind if I asked you about it?"

"Not much to tell. I was born with it, I think."

"I see. Well, I should be going now."

The detective stood and started for his car in the parking lot.

"Wait, Lawrence."

"Yes?"

"Am *I* a suspect?"

"Not at all. How could you be a suspect when the boy committed suicide?"

"That's what I thought. Please, tell his family I'm deeply sorry."

Lawrence said nothing as he opened the door to his car and sat in the driver's seat. He watched Gwendolyn gather her things and walk purposefully back to the bank. As he turned the key in the ignition a beam of light suddenly caught his eye. It was faint at first but as he followed it back to its source, it started to gain in strength. Gwen was standing there, jacket folded over her arms, smiling back at the detective. She waved briefly before disappearing into the darkness of the bank's lobby. That warm glow.... As Lawrence pulled out of the parking space, he obsessed over a sparkle so enchanting that he couldn't help but want to see it again.

*   *   *

Jeffery paced about his office. He peered down at his phone and let out a long, exhausted sigh. He'd already plugged a number into the phone, but he was perpetually hovering over the dial button. It had been almost a full day since their date, but Jeffery just couldn't get the vivacious bank teller out of his mind. He beamed when he imagined her smile and infectious laughter. He stared at his phone again.

I'll wait another day. I don't want her to think I'm some desperate fool.

Jeffery went back a screen and started to peruse his Facebook feed. The instant he started he wondered about Gwendy's Facebook account. What kind of things would be there? Did she follow anyone he knew, or maybe she liked to follow similar music groups. She did mention during dinner how much she loved music. Wait. She probably had a lot of admirers. Jeffery wanted to search Gwendolyn O'Hara but knew that he'd see thousands of men all pining, lovesick over her. He swallowed hard. Could he honestly deal with knowing she dated more than a few men casually? Jeffery put his phone back in his front pants pocket and sat down. He gazed up at the clock and immediately covered his face with one hand. He'd not been at work for more than two hours, and he still had seven more to go.

*   *   *

Lawrence returned to the precinct. He gave his file on the Sean Hammond case to the file clerk, a young woman with an extremely inappropriate low-cut dress and neon blue lipstick. Her chin-length platinum-blonde hair was streaked with black, which reminded Lawrence of a skunk.

"This case is closed. File it and get me anything outstanding from the last three days."

"Sure." She sauntered over to the desk, grabbed a couple of case files that had just come in and handed them to Lawrence. Her lips parted into a semisweet smile.

"These are from today, actually. First come, first serve."

Lawrence smiled back which felt more than forced. In his mind he'd already glimpsed the personification of beauty, grace and caring. All other smiles immediately felt as frigid and gruesome as the walk-in freezer in a slaughterhouse.

"I'm sorry, but could you try smiling a little more sincerely next time?"

"I'm sorry...." The annoyance wasn't hard to hear in the young woman's voice.

"When you smile at someone you should be more genuine or not do it at all. Christ! Is *everyone* just a fucking robot in this world?"

Lawrence pushed his way into the elevator, leaving the confused and insulted file clerk looking into her compact mirror for signs of geniality.

*   *   *

Jeffery pressed dial. The call was going through. A sweet female's voice answered.

"Hello?"

He wanted to talk but his brain scrambled to create words that weren't reaching his mouth. A terrible panic set in.

"Hello? Who is this?"

Jeffery could feel this mouth go dry and a thick sweat form on his brow. He felt his heart beat furiously, pounding against his chest like a jackhammer. He couldn't will the words to happen. The thoughts were there but they disappeared just as soon as they manifested, turning to ghosts and vanishing into the cobwebbed, dark attic that became this mind.

"Look, I can hear you breathing. If you don't want to say something, then at the very least hang up."

Jeffery ended the call and threw his cellular phone across the room in a fit of anger. He fell into the lounge chair and sunk into the leather as he fought to compose himself. His designer shirt was stuck to his body from a thick sweat. He couldn't get her out of his mind but he couldn't manage to speak with her either. He thought about going down to her work and paying her a visit. The thought immediately evaporated into the air. He smiled as he ran across the room to retrieve his phone. He quickly dialed a number.

The call was received by a pleasant-sounding gentleman.

"Ah, yes, I would like to send some flowers. I want the largest arrangement you carry."

"Okay, would that be for a wake or funeral?"

"Ah, no…. I want to send them to someone special."

"I see, sir. I suggest you go with one of our Degrees of Romance packages, then."

"What's the most expensive you have?"

"We have an arrangement for five hundred dollars, which includes a dozen roses of your choosing, a modest basket with scented bath products, and a box of assorted German chocolates."

"Good. I'll take that then!"

Jeffery's hands shook as he grabbed his credit card to read to the man on the other line. If this arrangement didn't convey his interest to Gwendy, then nothing would.

*   *   *

Gwendy prodded her salad with disinterest. She wasn't in the habit of going to the nearby shopping mall to eat at the food court, but she'd forgotten to make her lunch the night before. She picked up a lone grape tomato from her bowl and slowly bit into it. The juice was sweet and refreshing. She looked at the rest of the salad and pushed some lettuce leaves around with her plastic fork. There really were no more tomatoes. She frowned and dropped her uninteresting utensil into the bowl. She immediately got to her feet and strode over to the counter, where she'd ordered her food. The quick-service establishment, "Rooting for You," had slowed to a crawl since the initial lunch rush.

"Excuse me. This salad is not to my liking. I would have preferred more tomatoes, less lettuce and a lot more dressing. I don't wish to make a fuss, but may I have what *I* think is acceptable?"

The drowsy-looking boy behind the counter turned and paused as he made eye contact with the unsatisfied customer. He could not pull away from her gaze.

"Excuse me?" Gwendolyn continued, without the slightest wavering.

"Oh, I…. What did you want, ma'am?"

"I want more tomatoes, far less lettuce and more dressing in my salad. Oh, and may I also get some more of those cheddar cubes in my bowl as well? They were so good but gone too quickly. In this case, more is certainly better."

"Oh…. Those salads are premade in the back and sent up front. I don't have control over what they put in them."

"May I speak with someone who can comply with my order, then? I only wish to get what I paid for."

Gwen thrust the tray holding the salad into the boy's hands and folded her arms over her chest. Her smile was free and easy, displaying only warmth, but she wasn't going anywhere until she got what she wanted. It was obvious to anyone watching.

The sparkle in the woman's right eye was both alien and inviting. The boy behind the counter could feel himself being drawn to it.

"I'll go into the back and put together what you want. I'll just be a few minutes."

"I can wait. Thank you for your exemplary service. I really appreciate it!"

The boy lingered on Gwendolyn's smile a little longer before disappearing into the back to correct her order.

Gwen seized her cellphone and dialed out.

"Hello, Lawrence. This is Gwendolyn O'Hara. I've been wondering how the case with Sean Hammond is panning out. Oh, I see…. Well, that's a real shame. He was such a wonderful man. Anyway, are you available to grab a cup of coffee after work? Last night I remembered something about the evening Sean and I went out. It may be nothing but his behavior toward the end of our date seemed a little off. Perfect. Yes, I know the place. I'll see you then, and thank you so much for meeting with me. I'm looking forward to it, Detective. Oh, please, call me Gwendy."

The bank teller put her phone back in her purse and took out a notepad and pen. She scribbled something and handed it to the boy as he placed her freshly made salad on the counter.

"Please, give your supervisor this note for me. It details my experience here today, how much I appreciated you hearing out my complaint and then how you worked hard to rectify it. If they have any questions I penned my cellphone number on there so they should feel free to call me. I don't mind at all. This salad looks so yummy! Thank you."

Gwendy gathered up her lunch and went back to her quiet, corner table. She picked up a perfectly ripe grape tomato, generously covered in Italian dressing, and placed it into her mouth. A wave of euphoria washed over her as she squished the tomato and let the juices run down her throat.

*   *   *

Lawrence could feel the excitement as his shift was moments from its end. He grabbed his coat and whistled as he made his way to the front door. There was an extra-long stride in his step tonight.

"Larry! Don't check out yet. Someone just called in a 10-100 on the East Side. It could be a homicide. The person was *really* shaken up about what they saw."

"I've got plans. Can't you put someone else on it?"

"Everyone's maxed out on overtime as it is. Run this for me, and I'll try to get you out of there as soon as possible."

Lawrence had a surly grin on his face as he produced his cellphone from his pants pocket.

"You really owe me one."

He dialed Gwendy's number hoping to get her voicemail.

"Good evening, Lawrence. What's going on?"

Her voice was so sweet and perky. He instantly felt his mouth go dry and a small twinge of anxiety grasped his heart. It was like throwing a switch on a radio for volume.

"I, I… um… I was just asked to check out a possible homicide on the East Side of town."

"You won't be able to have coffee with me?" She sounded disappointed.

"No.… I was wondering if we could still meet, but after I check out the crime scene. Is that okay?"

"Sure it is. I'll just head home and get my laundry started up. What time do you think I should be at the coffee shop?"

"Give me at least two hours. I'll be there sooner if I can."

"Very well, I'll see you in a few hours, sir."

Lawrence ended the call. He couldn't explain the feeling, but it was almost as if he was actually worried about making Gwendolyn wait longer than necessary.

*　　*　　*

The police created a large blockade as a curious crowd teeming with questions was pushed aside. Lawrence produced his badge and walked right through the front door of the apartment building. This place was in the most expensive district of town. Most people could never dream of affording even a one-bedroom apartment on the East Side. The detective's final destination was a spacious two-bedroom with an impressive loft space. He looked around the apartment and took in the sights. Whoever this person was, they were very well off. He scoffed as he eyed a signed banner from his favorite hockey team prominently displayed on the wall. He'd been following the team his entire life and he couldn't afford the tickets to a single playoff game, yet this person had an official conference banner with all the players' signatures.

The smell inside the apartment was pungent but only enough to arouse suspicion. Kind of like when you suspect an animal has died under your house but can't quite verify it. Lawrence spied the body collapsed on the floor of the living room and instantly became pale. He quickly placed a handkerchief over his mouth, eyes wide with what could only be called shock. He'd seen a lot of disturbing crime scenes over the years but this one was horrific. This person had been tortured before being released from this world. Lawrence wasn't convinced that this was a homicide, though. However, if it weren't and all the wounds *were* self-inflicted then this man had been deeply troubled.

"What can you tell me?" Lawrence removed the handkerchief from around his mouth and addressed the lead forensics analyst. He took a small bottle of cologne out of his breast pocket and dabbed some on the handkerchief, deeply inhaling the scent.

"Okay. Judging by the spatter and placement of these tools, I'd have to conclude that our VIC did this to himself. This was all self-inflicted."

Lawrence bent low and examined the scene closer.

"So, it looks like we have a pair of slip-joint pliers, an electric hand tool with a rotary cutting bit, not unlike a circular saw blade, and a shoebox full of rubber tubing of some varying lengths and thicknesses. He did this to himself…. Our boy here sure knows his home-improvement tools. They look relatively new. Any receipts?"

"Nothing yet, and this is only preliminary but all the evidence points to suicide. We also found that circular tin next to the body. Why don't you take a look inside? Frankly, I think it's best that you see it for yourself."

Lawrence put on a pair of blue nitrile gloves and opened up the tin. Again he immediately raised his handkerchief to his face. The tin was a few inches deep and filled about halfway. Blood had pooled around most of the objects inside but there was no mistaking the contents.

"Make sure to match the skin, teeth and nails to our unfortunate, here. If there's even one mismatch then call me immediately. For all we know there could be another victim somewhere close. In my experience you don't cut on yourself to this degree without a reason."

Lawrence removed his gore-laden gloves and walked into the kitchen. He stopped. There was a bottle of rubbing alcohol on the table that was about a quarter full. It had a couple of pink smears around the top but they were faint.

"Did anyone mark this as evidence yet?"

An officer approached Lawrence. He was young.

"No, sir."

"For Heaven's sake! Bag it, but make sure you use gloves."

Lawrence had no doubt that the victim's fingerprints would be the only ones. The more he thought about it, the more sense a suicide was starting to make.

*   *   *

Gwen took a booth at the back of the café. She'd ordered a new concoction of pumpkin-and-cinnamon-flavored coffee and a poppyseed muffin. The muffin was warm, freshly baked. She took a sip of her drink and smiled as she tore off a piece of the muffin. She peered over to a couple sitting in the booth across from her. They were young, teenagers, who looked deeply into each other's eyes as they conversed. The girl looked absolutely smitten with her date as he imitated the look of a befuddled referee at a football game. Gwen sighed and went back to eating her muffin. If the date she bore witness to was anything like the ones she'd been on, then that girl would never hear from him again. Gwen pondered, then rose from her seat and walked over to the adjacent booth.

"Excuse me. I don't mean to intrude, but are you two on a date?"

The girl giggled, which seemed to be a nervous reaction. The boy was more composed and seemed best to answer the question.

"Yeah."

Gwendolyn smiled.

"And… do you like this girl?"

The question came out of nowhere like a sucker punch.

The young man was now positioned in the crosshairs of the girl sitting across from him. She looked expectantly at him with her arms folded over her chest.

"Well, yeah. Of course I do."

Gwendolyn nodded.

"I see. Well, if you do enjoy her company then please call her tomorrow. I can tell that she wants to see you again and it would be a shame if you decided that you, for some odd reason, didn't."

She turned on her heel and went back to her booth. The couple conversed again, but this time quieter and with more seriousness. Gwen, sitting alone in her booth and eating her baked goods, could only muse over the situation.

Suddenly, Gwendolyn got up and exited the café. She waved goodbye to the staff behind the counter and decided to turn off her phone as soon as her heels clacked against the street.

*   *   *

Lawrence had tried calling Gwendy's cellphone for the last hour. She wasn't at the coffee shop and every single call went directly to her voicemail. He had only left one message, nothing in the way of an inquisition, but he was starting to worry about her. Lawrence had looked up her home address so he could head over at any time. Was he overacting? He decided to pour himself a glass of bourbon and relax with the television until bed. However, he couldn't help but remain in a state of unrest. He switched channels until he found the hockey game, already in progress. As the puck bounced from perfect tape-to-tape passes, his mind raced. Lawrence got up from the sofa and checked his phone. There were no missed calls. The detective sighed. The sound of the game-winning goal echoed throughout the downstairs, but he didn't give it the slightest thought. It just didn't seem important.

*   *   *

Gwendolyn awoke to the sound of a jackhammer demolishing the street. She threw on her bathrobe and hurried to the front door. She swung it open and dashed across the street. The woman was still barefoot. The construction crew silently watched her as she approached.

"Excuse me, who's in charge here?" she shouted with a spike of frustration in her tone.

Still silent, an older gentleman with a dirty baseball cap and thick silver mustache stepped forward. He was about a few inches shorter than the woman, stocky and weathered.

"Could you please not start work until 9:00 A.M.? I have to be at work at 8:45 so it'll give me plenty of time to wake up in a pleasant manner and ensure that I treat the customers at the bank with the respect that they deserve. I mean, how would you feel if a bank teller scowled and barked at you because they didn't get a proper night's rest? Wouldn't it throw your entire day off?"

"Um… ma'am… I don't make the schedule. We were told to start this job before rush-hour traffic. We've been here for about an hour."

"Then please give me the name and contact number for the person who makes the schedule. I'm sure if I talk to them then they might be inclined to listen to reason."

"Um… okay, sure…."

All of the crew, confused and awestruck by this woman, remained silent as Gwen took a nondescript business card from the foreman and dashed back to her home. As she closed the door, a wry smile came over her face. Apparently a message had been left last night on her cellphone from Lawrence. Not answering his calls or showing him her presence had forced him to make the next move. The spectacular star in her right eye twinkled in the morning sun as she listened to the message not once but three times before calling the scheduler at city hall.

*　　*　　*

The apartment came up clean for prints, save for those of the victim. The forensics team rallied together to present their findings at the morning briefing. All the teeth, fingernails, toenails and skin slivers belonged to the owner of the apartment. He'd been found dead in the living room, but he'd begun his methodical, perverse work in the first-floor bathroom. He'd removed a large chuck of skin there but decided to do the rest of his self-mutilation in the living area. All evidence pointed to a severe act of masochism gone awry. He worked on himself, diligently and as precisely as possible, until he suffered a heart attack from the stress. The team estimated at least two hours of straight, uninterrupted abuse before the heart gave out.

A veteran detective rose from his chair and voiced his opinion.

"What if someone was making him do it? Like say our VIC had a gun trained on him and he'd had no choice but to comply?"

Lawrence decided that he'd squash that idea as soon as it escaped the other detective's lips.

"We have no witnesses who can put someone else at this man's apartment. In fact, the people who live in the building said he'd hadn't left for several days. Also, why make him put all his pieces in a tin if you weren't going to take it as some kind of trophy? No, the disturbing thing is that this man decided to do this to himself and leave a collection box for us to find. Did anyone check into his profession?"

No one answered but all eyes were focused on Lawrence.

"Well, I did. For someone with a law degree he cuts better than my butcher."

A short woman wearing thin-framed glasses spoke up. Her brown hair was swept back into a tight ponytail. Lawrence recognized her as one of the forensics team who specialized in toxins and other cooked-up chemical compounds. She was very good at her job so he gave her his full attention.

"What if this was *more* than just some guy mutilating himself. Perhaps he was doing it for someone else. Let's think outside the box here, no pun intended. Say that the tin was intended for someone… someone whom he deemed special. Maybe his offering was exactly that, but he never got to send it to the intended person. If we're going off this assumption then it wouldn't be farfetched to assume the intended is a woman or maybe even a man that the deceased was very interested in winning over."

The theory was sound but Lawrence just couldn't accept that someone would actually go to such extremes just to get another person's attention. Was the act of love so difficult for Jeffery Saunders to express that he needed to reach into a darkness so deep that it was bottomless?

The entire room was filled with low, muffled voices. Lawrence decided to slip out of the morning briefing and check in on Gwendolyn. The case had him intrigued but Gwendolyn was still not answering his calls, and this was proving to be more of a problem than he could handle.

"Hey. I was wondering if I would hear from you today or not." Her voice was as pleasant as the sound of a jazz pianist in the midst of an impromptu solo. The detective could listen to that sweetly pretty rising intonation forever if she'd allowed him.

"Oh, hey.… I thought you were angry with me. I mean… I hope I didn't offend you or anything."

"Not at all. I just needed some time to think without any distractions last night. So, how was the crime scene, Detective? Was it a homicide?"

"I'm starting to think it might have been an accidental death, maybe even a suicide. Only the victim's prints in the apartment and no sign of forced entry or foul play."

"Suicide? That sounds horrific. Would you mind if I asked what happened?"

"I don't think you'll want to hear this one, Gwendolyn. A smile as beautiful as yours doesn't need a reason to turn into a doleful frown. Trust me, your customers at the bank will thank me."

"Ah, so you *have* been thinking about my smile, Mister! Sounds like I've been on your mind."

"You could say that. So, would you be open to try meeting me again? Let me make things up to you for not being at the coffee shop on time."

"Okay. I think we should have dinner tomorrow night. How about you pick me up at 8, after my shift?"

"I'd like that."

"Good. I'll see you then."

Gwendolyn hung up her phone. A smile from ear to ear was etched into her preened, porcelain skin. This *new* tactic was working very well. Not only did Lawrence seem interested but he'd had already gotten up the nerve to call her several times. Maybe being a detective made him more intuitive than the other men? She happily mused to herself.

She sauntered back to her booth, smoothing her purple miniskirt with both hands before sitting down and crossing her left leg over her right. She was about to light her available sign when a newspaper fell down upon the counter in front of her. She looked over to see her coworker, Rose, with a very serious look to her face. The woman's normally tan complexion was completely drained of color. Gwendolyn placed a hand on Rose's bony shoulder and pulled her close.

"Hey there. Are you okay, sweetie?" She rubbed and caressed the joint with strong, soothing fingers.

"You mean you don't know? Look at the paper." The whisper was almost choked off by tears.

The bold headline was impossible to ignore.

Prominent Prosecutor Jeffery Saunders found dead in his apartment.

Gwen's eyes widened. *Another one?* She gasped and turned to face Rose. "He killed himself?"

Rose nodded. "The police aren't saying yet but his body was only discovered yesterday. It had been a while since Mr. Saunders came in. In fact, I haven't seen him since the day he asked you out, Gwendy."

"Yeah…. We had a good time…. However, despite having a good time I never heard from him afterward. I thought maybe he'd found someone more interesting and decided to come to the bank on the days I had off to avoid running into me."

"That makes *two* men who have died who frequently came to our bank. The weird part is that they both went on dates with you at one point or another."

"Wait…. Are you implying that I had something to do with their deaths, Rose? I'm deeply offended that you would even think that. I thought we were friends." Gwen's smile faded and was replaced by a very somber, dark mask.

Rose looked away for an instant. She made sure to meet Gwendy's gaze before she next spoke.

"Actually, I wasn't accusing you of anything. I was just going to point out that the police might stop by and question you about him, seeing as how you two went out and all. I wanted to tell you that if you needed to talk then I'm here for you, Gwendy."

"Oh." Gwendolyn perked up instantly, the dark mask cracking under the pressure of high cheekbones and soft laugh lines. "You're very sweet to offer but I think I'll be okay. I only went out with him once, after all. It's not like I was emotionally invested or anything."

"Okay. Well…."

"What is it, Rose?"

"Nothing. I'm just getting in so I better get my station ready."

Gwendolyn watched her colleague intently as she slowly walked back to her counter. She made note of the uneasiness in her movements as well as the tension between them only moments ago. Gwen felt she wasn't wrong in assuming that Rose suspected she had something to do with the death of Jeffery Saunders. In what universe did a date normally end in death days later? The redhaired clerk sat down again and put on her light. She took a deep breath, let it out and smiled as bright and inviting as ever.

*   *   *

Lawrence went through Jeffery Saunders's personal belongings. He wasn't just anyone. He was a very wealthy attorney who'd also done quite well in the stock market. He'd made a killing in the market last year, enough to buy an impressive condo on the East Side and a newly renovated beach house. The detective picked up a thin cellphone. He scrolled through the call history. There was a recurring number that seemed to be the focus of his attention up until his death. Lawrence recalled the death of Sean Hammond, who'd also had an unhealthy obsession with making frequent calls to Gwen's number before *his* death. The call log matched up almost identically, but the recurring number didn't belong to Gwen. Lawrence grabbed a pen and paper and wrote down the number. It looked local. He continued to look through the evidence bin. When he pulled the plastic-bagged pair of slip-joint pliers from the box, he winced as he recalled their application. The burly detective sighed and placed his hands behind his head. He circled the room. His strides slowed as he found himself lost in thought.

If I call the number, I might find out who he was trying to contact before his death.

The call went straight to a voice recording from a muted woman proclaiming that the mailbox for this person was full. Lawrence continued to rifle through Jeffery's call log until he spied a familiar business number.

It was the number to a florist, which Lawrence used on several occasions to send flowers to the families of deceased officers. He called the number and waited patiently for someone to answer.

"Hello. This is Arrangements by Amy."

"Um, hi. My name is Detective Lawrence Stowell."

"Oh! Hello, Detective. Will you need an arrangement for a wake or funeral?"

"Um… *no*. Who the hell is this?"

"It's Michael. I always assist you with your arrangements. The last one I did for you was three months ago to the Rodriguez family. I recall clearly that you requested we include yellow roses in the mix because they were his wife's favorite flower."

"Oh, right… Michael…. Yeah, I'm sorry… I'm just… I guess I do a lot of orders through Amy, huh?"

"I'll say you do. It's a terrible shame that they always have to be for those in mourning. Anyhow, how can I assist you?"

"Would you be able to look up a customer of yours for me? He might have used Amy to send flowers or maybe a gift basket. It's for a case I'm working."

"Sure. Do you know if he ordered from us frequently?"

"No. I only have a one suspected instance. I found this number in his cellphone. The call was almost a half-hour long so I'm assuming he ordered something."

"What's the customer's name?"

"Jeffery Saunders. Saunders is spelled S-A-U-N-D-E-R-S."

"Okay. I'll look him up as soon as I have a free minute and give you a call back when I find out what he ordered."

"Specifically, I'd like to know to whom and where the arrangement was sent."

"Okay. I have three large orders to fill so is it alright if I get back to you later? I'm kind of a one-man show today."

"That'll be fine, Michael."

"Talk to you soon, Detective."

*   *   *

Gwendolyn looked behind her at the arrangement of beautiful flowers that Jeffery Saunders had sent her. Some of the blooms were starting to wilt. She'd kept up with the maintenance, but inside the bank, the flowers were only destined to shrivel up and die. The realization of their eventual demise certainly expressed how fragile life can be. Plucking a flower from its natural environment to live out borrowed time in a vase almost seemed wrong now. She carefully picked up the vase and went into the breakroom. Gwen took the remaining roses out and wrapped them in some paper towel. She dumped the water in the vase out in the sink and placed it, empty, on the breakroom table. The blue-and-green crystal made a nice centerpiece. Rose was seated near the windows with the blinds closed. She was quietly enjoying a cup of coffee out of a large white mug.

"You know, it *is* a lovely day. Why don't we open these blinds and let some light in?"

Rose only nodded in acknowledgment of Gwendolyn's statement.

The blinds slowly rose up, revealing the outside world in a glorious blinding flash. Rose had turned away and held a hand over the tops of her eyes while Gwen reveled in the splendid warmth of the sun's rays as they filtered in through the glass. The world beyond was a silent movie.

"You know, it can be dangerous to look at the sun. It's *so* beautiful but the exposure of UV light to your skin and eyes for too long can cause all kinds of terrible things. I've read extensive studies on the subject matter."

Rose brought her cup to her lips. She was watching as the redhaired beauty only seemed to transform like a blooming rose reaching up to the sun for love and inspiration. She wanted to look away but couldn't. The sight was mesmerizing. She'd never noticed before exactly how beautiful Gwen truly was. She wondered if Gwen knew.

Gwendolyn looked over to Rose, who seemed to be in a trance. "Is everything okay?"

Rose nodded. "I guess I never realized it before, but there's a sparkle about you… something so inviting that I just can't look away."

Gwen blushed. "Rose! You're embarrassing me."

"I mean it. Can I ask you about your right eye?"

"What would you like to know?"

"How is it so unique, so lovely?"

"I was born with it this way. Unfortunately, this is the only answer I have for you."

"It's very unusual, pretty."

"Rose! What a way to insult my left eye!" The trilling of Gwen's laughter was as refined as birdsong.

"No, I'm sorry…. I didn't mean anything like that about your left eye."

"Well, I need to get back out on the floor, Rose." She touched the woman's hand and watched as Rose followed the lines of her fingers, to her shoulder and over to her face, which beamed exquisitely in the sun's golden glow. The effect of the sun on Gwendolyn's skin made it appear like brilliant moonlight was seeping out from her very pores. Her porcelain fairness only seemed to brighten that which it absorbed.

"I'm very sorry I said what I said earlier, Rose. Everyone always expects the worst of others so much so that I guess I became defensive. It was wrong to categorize you with them. Those men were special and I sincerely feel terrible that they committed suicide. Believe me, I wish they were still alive, healthy and flirting with me at my counter. This is how I'll always remember them, you know?"

"You seemed to like them both a lot. I'm sorry I came off sounding like a bitch. I wasn't accusing you of anything, Gwendy. The coincidence just struck me as a little odd."

"I know. Just stay and enjoy the sun. I'll be on the floor, envious." Gwendolyn giggled and left Rose in front of the large breakroom windows.

Rose wanted to watch the sun all day. For some strange reason, this idea was the most appealing one she'd ever had.

*   *   *

Gwen managed to finish up earlier than expected at the bank. This extra time would allow her to pop into one of the nearby stores to look for a new dress. She was going out with Lawrence tomorrow night so the thought of a new outfit really made her excited. Something subtle but sexy—enough to show off but not show all. This excitement was entirely new to Gwendolyn. Sure, she'd felt twinges of excitement course through her body both before and during her last few dates but nothing akin to this. A new experience deserved a new outfit.

The small boutique across from the firehouse sold some tasteful high-end fashionable clothing. Gwendolyn had peeked inside a few times but the price tags violently chased her out of the store wielding pitchforks and torches. Today would be different, though. She walked in, confidently, and immediately closed the ground between her and the dress rack. There was a perfect single-file line of cute dresses parading around the store.

She chose a black silk one with emeralds beading the neckline and a slit up the right leg. It had everything she could possibly want. She shut her eyes for a moment and reached for the tag at the shoulder strap. It brandished a flaming stick aimed at her modest paycheck.

The store clerk walked over to her. She was a petite woman with a small face and crooked nose. She almost looked more like a bird than a human being.

"You have exquisite taste. That'd look great with your complexion and body type."

Gwendolyn smiled and insecurely stared at the price tag again. She could still feel the heat.

"Why don't you try it on? You might get a better feeling about it once you've seen it on you."

Gwen nodded and made her way over to the dressing room. She went inside and locked the door.

A few minutes later she called out from behind the door.

"Excuse me. Would you mind terribly if I could try on a pair of black heels with this? My flats aren't really working, and I'd really like to have the full effect before making a decision. I'm a size seven."

A box slid under the door with a pair of suede two-inch heels inside. Gwendolyn slipped into them and emerged from the changing area.

The clerk and two other customers in the store stared in awe. She was absolutely perfect. The dress looked as though it had been made just for Gwen. The silk lovingly hugged her bosom and hips and the slit at the right leg showed everything up to her thigh. She admired herself in the mirror, giving a subtle twirl to make sure her butt didn't look too big in the dress. It seemed to be working with her amicably. Gwendolyn turned back towards the store clerk.

"Do you think this dress would impress a man on a first date? Please, be honest with me."

"Are you kidding? It looks amazing on you! Whoever he is, he's a lucky man."

"Really?" Gwendy strutted around the store and caught glimpses of herself in the wall mirror at different angles. She still seemed skeptical.

"If *you* were a man and I came outside wearing this dress, would *you* expect something more from me?"

"I'm not sure I understand. What're you asking?"

"Does the dress make me look like I have reasonably priced virtue?"

"You mean… does it make you look like a prostitute?"

"Whoa! Hey, there! Let's not resort to name-calling. I'm just looking to send the right signals during my date."

"What signal are you trying to send?"

"Hmm… well… how about that I'm interested. Yeah. I'm interested, and I want him to be interested too. However, even though I'm interested I'm not going to do anything scandalous on a first date."

"Trust me, girl, he'll be interested, and I'm pretty sure on his hands and knees ready to lick the soles of your shoes if you dare ask."

"Ewww, no. I think that sounds absolutely abhorrent. But you've convinced me to take the dress. Please bag it up and I'll come by on my lunch break tomorrow."

"Okay. You'll need to leave a deposit to do that."

"That's not what it says on the layaway plan posted on the register counter. It states here that I can have you hold the dress for me for exactly twenty-four hours before I pay anything."

"Normally I would say that's correct but this is a designer dress and the last one in the shop. If someone else wants it and will pay for it right then and there, then I can guarantee nothing."

"Is that so? I chose this overly priced boutique because it has something that I want. If you can't give me that, then I suggest you call your manager."

"Look, I *am* the manager here! If you want this dress then you need to put some cash or credit down first."

Gwen tilted her head slightly to the left. She was starting to become annoyed but a wave of rationality began to wash over her. She stared back at her opposition and decided that it was time to play nice.

"Okay. Since I can't have this dress without a down payment, how much do you require?"

"A third of the total cost will hold it for you."

"Fine." Gwendolyn brandished a credit card and forcefully handed it to the clerk. "Charge it."

The avian bobbed her head as she ran the card.

The transaction went through and Gwendolyn smiled as she received her card back.

"I'll be back on my lunch break tomorrow. For that much money should I expect this to be giftwrapped with platinum bows?"

The clerk scoffed and handed Gwen the receipt. She stopped for a brief moment and admired the sparkle in Gwendolyn's right eye. It was like a ball of fire screaming inside the infinite darkness of a volcano. It was so warm.

"You have a very unique eye. It's *so* beautiful! Is it cosmetic?"

"No. I was born with it like this. Do you think I should do something to cover it up? A lot of people think it's so unusual that they simply stare and it kind of embarrasses me."

"No! I wouldn't do anything like that at all! You should flaunt it."

"Well, maybe.... Thank you for the compliments. I'll be back tomorrow as I stated earlier. Please have the dress bagged, and I'd like it steamed and ready to wear. I won't have time to give it that kind of attention so I'm going to leave that burden to you. Is it alright?"

"Yes. I'll make sure to treat it for you."

"Excellent. See you tomorrow."

Gwendolyn stepped onto the street. The sun was beginning to go down and she loved the scarlet hues mixing with the purple of the sky. It was as though someone spilled red paint on a dark canvas and haphazardly swirled it in. She watched as an ambulance and two police cars turned the corner right at the fire station. They were in a hurry, lights flashing and sirens blaring. She smiled and set off to the parking garage, where she'd left her car for the day.

It's so nice to see that our city's appointed protectors are always doing their job, making haste to save lives. I hope they make it in time so that I can read all about the daring rescue in the papers tomorrow.

*   *   *

Lawrence arrived back at his apartment. He'd not cleaned in a few days so it was no surprise when he encountered a contingent of warriors dressed up in Chinese takeout containers ready to lay siege to the countertops and eventually take over the small dining room. He picked up the large garbage bag on the floor and started to sweep his foes into its dark depths. He sighed when he realized that no matter how much he cleaned, it would never look impressive enough for someone like Gwendolyn. She was used to men with lots of money, boyish looks, brazen and charming. Lawrence was stocky, more sarcastic than charming, and completely lackluster. He enjoyed his scotch and whiskey. He liked to watch the hockey games and devour his meals from out of a paper or plastic container—his perfectly spotless stove a testament to his eating habits. He dropped the bag and sat down in his favorite Barca Lounger. He picked up the section of the paper with the crossword he'd been doing yesterday, still unfinished. Lawrence was a fan of puzzles. He looked at one of the empty sets of boxes. With his pen he wrote the word that matched the clue. That was Lawrence for you. He'd always be the kind of man that did his crosswords in pen.

*   *   *

"It was simply awful, Gwendy. You should've seen her."

Gwendolyn paced around the kitchen with her cellphone pressed to her ear. She was listening intently to the woman on the other end.

"What do you mean? I *had* seen her that day. She seemed fine to me."

"No… not then… I mean, she looked awful. Her lips were all dry and cracked, bleeding a little too. She just *refused* to leave that window. It was just so weird."

"What did the paramedics have to say after she was taken into the ambulance?"

"Severely dehydrated and some first-degree burns on her face and neck. I'm telling you, though, it was like she was in some sort of trance, Gwendy. She started screeching like a banshee when they removed her from that window. I didn't even know she had the lungs to make such tortured sounds for that long. She really frightened me."

"Will she be alright?"

"She should be. She's at the hospital overnight for observation."

"Can she have visitors?"

"Not tonight. Maybe tomorrow, I don't know, though."

"I think I'll stop in before my shift. I'd go in the evening but I have a previous engagement."

"You're such a good friend, Gwendy. I'm sure she'll appreciate you coming to see her. Rose always speaks so highly of you."

"That's very sweet of you to say, Janice, but I'm only doing what she'd do for me. I *will* give her your best. See you tomorrow."

Gwendolyn ended the call, silently standing in the kitchen. She was lost in thought. She turned on her heel and started for her bedroom. All that mattered was going to see Rose in the morning before her shift. She slipped on a pair of tiny pink shorts. They were very comfortable. A matching camisole glided over her head and fitted itself down to her midriff. Gwendolyn sat down at her vanity and began brushing her lustrous hair. She eyed her cellphone as it skittered across the glass top of the vanity. It was a text message from Lawrence. With a smile even wider than normal she replied and went back to the task of spinning straw to silk. She couldn't help but keep that smile plastered on her fair face. Even asleep she imagined that it would stay with her all night long.

*   *   *

The nurse led Gwendolyn down a long corridor in the psychiatric ward of the hospital. People gathered to watch the redhaired angel who practically glided down the hallway instead of walked. They hollered and gasped as Gwen purposefully made her way to the room of Rosario Alma. Rose was sitting erect in her bed just staring out the window. She had a melancholic expression on her face like she was searching for something that just wasn't there anymore.

"You have a visitor here, Ms. Alma."

"Nurse… why can't you move me to one of the rooms that face the sun? All I can see are these ugly dark clouds and shadows. Is it going to rain again *this* hour too?"

The nurse turned to Gwen and whispered, "She doesn't seem cognizant that the clouds are from an oncoming storm only a few hours out. She believes that it's been raining on and off all day long and that *we're* keeping her away from the sun on purpose."

Gwendolyn nodded and placed a reassuring hand on the nurse's shoulder.

"I will be fine with her alone. Rose and I are very close and I'm certain she would never harm me."

"Okay.…. If there's a problem, there's a call button on the side of the bed. Be gentle with her, dear."

Gwendolyn folded her spring jacket on a nearby chair and sat on the bed facing Rose. Rose looked up for an instant but quickly shied away from Gwendy. There was some visible agitation. Gwen smiled and reached for one of Rose's hands. Rose pulled away and folded her arms over her chest, softly rocking back and forth, muttering to herself.

"What's wrong? Are you upset about something, Rose? We're best friends. You can tell me."

"You… why can't you just leave? You've been here all night long. Just go away and leave me alone."

"If that is what you want then I will not object."

Gwen reached for her jacket when a hand clasped her wrist. It was like a vice. She followed the hand to a wide-eyed Rose, who was practically in tears. She shivered violently. Gwen steeled herself and sat back down. She let out a long breath and fixed her work colleague with a sweet smile.

"Please. Please bring back the sun, Gwendy. I know you took it away but I won't tell anyone. Just give it back. Please?" The look in Rose's eyes was that of pure desperation.

"And what would you tell them exactly, Rose? Would you say that I took the sun away from you because I was some sort of spiteful child?"

"I would tell them the truth! You stole it because you knew I wanted it! That sun was so warm and shined so brightly but you couldn't have that. You snuffed it out like it was nothing!"

"Now, now, Rose. You're not making much sense at all. The sun has always been there. It just needed to go away for a while, but it will come back."

"No! You murdered it! Murderer!" The shriek in her voice was more animal than human.

Gwendolyn backed up a little. She ripped her wrist away from the vice that was holding it. Her eyes, which normally shone like two semiprecious gems, were overwhelmed by ire.

"How dare you? I can only imagine your pain, but to call me such a heinous word makes me question how much I mean to you."

"Well, it's true. You murdered the sun and now you want me to wallow in the darkness, but I'll not allow you to do that to me. I know your game. I'll find a way to beat you."

Gwen continued to smile at Rose. She seemed to detect something droll laced together with the insanity coming from out of Rose's mouth. Rose immediately became irritated.

"Why are you laughing? Stop it! I'm going to win!"

Gwendolyn continued to laugh. Her misplaced mirth was causing Rose to rock aggressively in her bed.

"I said to stop it! Stop mocking me, Gwendy!"

"Oh, Rose. You are a funny one. I wanted to believe that I could be the one to help you— that you weren't truly lost. Despite everything, I think I still *can* help you. Would you like me to help you, Rose?"

Rose burst into a sobbing fit. She absently pulled out a chunk of her hair but continued as if she'd never done it.

"Please… please help me, Gwendy. I'm so scared…."

Gwendolyn sat back on the bed and held Rose close to her. Her lips gently brushed against Rose's ear. The feel of Gwendolyn's skin made Rose fold into her friend even more. She was starting to feel safe in Gwen's arms— the feeling not unlike when her mother held her as an infant.

Gwendolyn whispered something delicately into Rose's ear. Rose immediately backed away, staring in awe at her friend and colleague. The woman began to display a serene smile as Gwen nodded her head in a positive gesture. Rose stayed pensive no longer. She sank into the warmth of the bed and faced the windows, tears silently streaming down her round cheeks.

Gwen picked up her jacket, slipped into it and walked out of the room. Only the rhythmic clack of the woman's heels sounded as she walked down the long hallway. Rose could feel the strength and conviction of the words whispered into her ear only moments ago. She started to giggle.

Gwendolyn passed the nurse who brought her down to Rose's room. The nurse ran to her.

"Wait! So, how did everything go? Did Rose take to you?"

"I think that she *really* did. I feel my presence here showed her what's important."

"I'm so glad. You're such a good friend to come down here for her like this. I don't think anyone else has bothered to visit her since her admittance."

"Thank you, but I didn't come here for praise. Rose is hurting. I hope my visit has truly been the healing elixir that she needs. She was rather docile when I left the room. Let's hope she has a good day."

"What did you say to her?" The nurse seemed to be in complete awe.

"I simply told her that the sun was never gone. I think it's all that she needed to hear."

"Oh, I see…. Well, thank you so much for brightening her day."

Gwendolyn continued to the parking lot. The humid air seeped into her lungs and she mused that rain wasn't too far off somewhere close by. She looked up at the windows where she imagined Rose to be at this very moment. She spied her waving to Gwendolyn from her room. Rose looked so happy. Gwen waved back.

*   *   *

The rhythmic tick-tock was starting to grate on Gwendolyn's nerves. For a while she clicked her tongue against her cheek to keep time but eventually fell out of synch. The bank teller felt like every single hour was divided into an eternity upon the hands of the giant wall clock. She also found it cruel that though there was a smaller clock behind the tellers that the larger one on the far wall grinned sadistically at them all day long. It was a constant reminder that her shift wasn't over yet. She still smiled and greeted every single customer but her smile couldn't have been more false. Gwen had picked her dress up from the boutique about thirty minutes ago and all she could think about was putting it on. She imagined that Lawrence would compliment her in a very shy way and that she'd think it was cute. As her next customer put down a deposit slip on her counter with a large sum of money, Gwen tried her best to seem interested. Unfortunately money and deposit slips would only be interesting if they suddenly came to life and performed a medley of showtunes. She took the transaction and looked up at her patron. He smiled at her but all she could manage was to quirk the left side of her mouth up enough to show a couple of teeth. If it were anyone else at the bank but her giving this expression then the man would feel insulted.

*   *   *

The police database came up empty. Lawrence hadn't heard anything from Michael so he passed the time looking for patterns or irregularities in Jeffery Saunders' behavior, hoping that maybe the man had a checkered past. He was squeaky clean. He received a parking ticket two years ago but it was paid promptly. There was no history of mental illness with neither him nor anyone else in his family. It was looking more and more likely that Jeffery Saunders had just, one fateful day, decided to mutilate himself for no apparent reason.

Lawrence drummed his fingers on the desk and thought about the case. The recurring number from his cell log turned out to be another dead end. Could the supposed gift, from Arrangements by Amy, that Jeffery sent *really* lead Lawrence to an acceptable conclusion as to why he took his life in such a violent manner? The case was starting to look more and more circumstantial and unexplainable at best.

Unexplainable?

The detective thought about it in those terms. Maybe there was a different pattern? He typed something into the search bar and waited. His eyes, half closed only a moment ago, forced open. There were a lot of men over the last few years who'd had committed suicide. This list! It was as though his keywords were deliberately slapping him in the face. Lawrence had searched unexplained suicides involving males in their 20s or 30s. The results were quite disturbing. He clicked on a link to a local paper write-up from a city about five hours away by car. The headlines went on to talk about a rash of suicides, involving four different men that were almost too gruesome to put in a public paper. These men were all successful and very influential—no notes left behind and no witnesses to foul play either. Lawrence went back to the national database and pulled up the case file on one of the deaths. He nearly lost his lunch as soon as the first set of crime scene photos loaded onto the screen. Lawrence had seen a lot of things in his time on the force but this was something he just couldn't prepare himself for.

The deceased had used a straight-edge razor to cut identical circular patterns on himself but this wasn't the actual cause of death. Apparently, he'd decided to tear his own eyes out using an icepick and a pair of hose-clamp pliers. That kind of trauma should've been etched on this man's dying face. It should've been the grimmest of Halloween masks, but the deceased looked completely at peace. Lawrence zoomed in closer on the man's face. He could make out some softer lines around the mouth denoting a smile or something close to it. The detective shrunk back in horror. Jeffery Saunders had had this same look. Sean Hammond, on what was left of his face, had a similar visage. The similarities in the stories were starting to look eerily familiar. Lawrence scribbled some notes and looked down at his watch. Despite the macabre scene displayed on his monitor, he still managed to whistle an upbeat tune before he grabbed his overcoat and exited the precinct for the evening.

*   *   *

Gwendolyn enjoyed Lawrence's company more so than she ever expected. He was sarcastic, having a more mordant sense of humor, but also very sweet. There was an honesty about him that was very refreshing. He wasn't trying to impress her with his wealth or power. Lawrence was just Lawrence, and that's all there was to it. Truthfully, it was nice to go to dinner with a man and not have to hear about his vacation houses, multiple sports cars or yacht. He lived modestly and that, in itself, was enough for a man like him to feel content.

Gwen intently watched him from across the table as he struggled with some chopsticks to pick up his cold noodles. He'd been at this for about five minutes.

"Do you need help or require a manual for that?" Her laughter was sprightly and saccharine-coated even as she playfully mocked him.

"This isn't as easy as it looks." Lawrence's frustration was not hidden.

"Here, let me show you how, Detective."

One minute she was sitting across from him at the table and the next she was standing to the right of him. Lawrence never even heard her move. She was quieter than a mouse. Gwen took his hand in hers and with her other hand she arranged the sticks to be in the correct position. She smiled the entire time. She sat down next to him and gestured for him to try his luck again. The sticks fell out of his hand before he managed to touch the plate. They both laughed loudly at the sight.

"I thought you had experience with this, Lawrence," she managed through her hysterics.

"I said I liked to eat Chinese food out of a carton. This is different. I feel like I'd do a better job with a spatula."

The laughing subsided as they both centered themselves on one another. Her beauty was absolutely mesmerizing, and his honesty was unbelievably infectious. Gwen held her smile just a little longer as Lawrence excused himself from the table. She couldn't help but desire him to come back as soon as possible.

*   *   *

The couple stood in the doorway outside of Gwendolyn's apartment. Lawrence couldn't remove his gaze from his date. He could easily say she was the most beautiful woman he'd ever seen. She rubbed a hand on his cheek, gently. The weathered skin felt nice under her smooth, silken skin.

"Thank you for dinner tonight. It's been a while since I have felt this comfortable with a man, or anyone else for that matter."

"It was my pleasure. May we do it again? Well… what I mean is, can I see you again?"

Gwen laughed. "Does that mean you are *done* seeing me now?" She stood on the tips of her toes and leaned in.

Lawrence met her lips with his in a passionate kiss that caused Gwendolyn to throw her slender arms around his neck. The detective rested his strong hands on her waist. His touch felt trained. She pulled back and stared into his eyes. She could feel his desire. It was palpable—real. Gwendolyn never felt this sensation from any other man before. Sure, she was without doubt that the others were interested, but this was something else. She liked it.

"Would you like to come in?"

"I… well, I would but…." He spoke softly and his husky voice only added to Gwendolyn's attraction to him.

"Lawrence. Please come in?"

He nodded in approval as she produced her keys from her purse.

Gwendolyn led him to the living room couch. She let him sit down on the middle cushion as she slid her jacket over her shoulders and down her body until it fell listlessly to the floor. Gwendolyn reached behind her back and removed the clasp at the top of the dress and pulled the zipper all the way down. She climbed on top of Lawrence and started kissing his wide neck.

Lawrence let out a satisfied moan as she focused on his collar bone and pawed at his dress shirt. She was unbuttoning his shirt with sure strokes. Lawrence eased the fabric of her dress down. He watched the fabric bunch and roll easily over her breasts, stopping at her hips. He cupped those breasts gently with his large hands, which were supple yet still firm—perfect. She giggled with great delight as she ran her fingertips over his bare chest and shoulders. His cologne held the fragrance of the ocean foaming upon the shore—the saltiness blending with the sharp contrast of the sand beneath, smoothing it to perfection with wave after wave. Lawrence's face was shaved only a few hours ago but the skin had a roughness that Gwendolyn found more than appealing. She noted that this was not a mere boy but a man in her home.

Lawrence's hands slid around her buttocks and held her firmly. She let out a tiny, breathy cry of satisfaction – eyes glassy from desire. Gwen could feel the strength of his fingers as they dug into her apple hip. She dropped her hands lower to unfasten his belt and the buttons on his slacks.

She kissed him passionately, biting down slightly on his lip once more, and slowly pulled away.

She stood and pushed the dress down to the floor with a single wiggle of her hips. Gwen was clad in only her high-cut black satin panties and heels. She stared hungrily at her date. She knew she wanted him tonight. It had to be tonight.

"So, would you like to take the rest of this activity to the bedroom?"

"Are you sure?"

"Yes. Aren't you?"

Lawrence hesitated for a moment. She was beautiful in every single way a woman could be. Gwendolyn was every man's fantasy made flesh, and yet Lawrence found himself wondering if this was the right thing to do.

"This is a little fast for me. My wife died five years ago, and you're the first woman I've been out with since. I know this sounds really stupid right now. I mean, you could have anyone you want and here I am practically looking for an excuse to run home to a cold shower."

Gwen pouted for a second. She rolled her panties down to her hips and pushed them to the floor. Her smile was as warm as a hearth in the middle of a cold, winter's night. Lawrence felt himself being drawn into that warmth with every second. Gwendolyn took his cold hands in hers and led him from the couch to the blaze of her bedroom.

It has to be tonight.

"Look, Lawrence, we don't have to if you feel you would rather not, but I desire you. I swell with anticipation for you to fill me up. I have never felt like this with another man before. They are always so brash and verbose, bragging all night about their achievements and throwing money around like it'll make me fall for them, but that only makes them more transparent and lackluster to me. Your modesty and kind heart have won my affections. A truer gentleman I cannot imagine. Please, make love to me this night. It must be tonight!"

Even if he could have said no, his heart decidedly spoke yes. Lawrence simply couldn't refuse such an offer. He felt himself lost within the scarlet waves of her hair and the touch of silk that was her body. He held her close and breathed deep of her scent. She smelled of cherry licorice and daisies. Her moonlit skin made *his* look so dark in contrast. He moved his hands over the small of her back and she rose to meet his lips again.

The two lovers collapsed on the bed and became one.

*   *   *

Morning came and a very satisfied Lawrence rolled over to edge of the bed. He pulled his cellphone from his pants pocket. He'd missed a call from Arrangements by Amy last night. He watched over the perfect naked form of Gwendolyn, who slept so soundly. She seemed translucent as the morning sun filtered in through her blinds bathing her in the glow of warm sunlight.

Lawrence put his pants on and quietly left the bedroom to return the call. Gwendolyn stirred.

She got up and followed Lawrence out the door of the bedroom. She'd borrowed his shirt from the floor and threw it on.

Lawrence raised the phone to his ear and felt the familiar embrace of lithe but strong arms wrapping around his waist. He instantly smiled.

"I'm going to make us breakfast. How do you take your eggs?"

"I don't normally take my eggs on anything." The gruff voice held that sarcasm that Gwendolyn found so enticing.

"Okay, Detective. How about I surprise you, then?" Her lilt was cut short by a small yawn as her hands slid away from his stomach.

Lawrence's eyes followed her into the kitchen as she grabbed for a frying pan and some essentials from the refrigerator. The detective almost forgot that he'd called anyone.

"Hello? I said this is Arrangements by Amy. Can I help you?"

"Oh, um… good morning, Michael. This is Lawrence. Sorry that I missed your call last night. I had a late date."

"Oh, hello, Lawrence. Am I wrong to suspect that this late date went very well?"

"No, not at all. You're very perceptive. So, what do ya have for me?"

"The arrangement you asked about was delivered to a Gwendolyn M. O'Hara at the bank. I also have a copy of the card that was sent. Would you like to hear it?"

Lawrence felt his mouth go dry instantly. "Um, yes. Please tell me."

"'Dearest Gwendy. I haven't been able to get you out of my mind. It's like a fire burning deep inside my chest has suddenly turned to a blaze. You've captured my heart. Please accept this offering.'"

The detective turned his head and spied his lovely dove still cooking with a smile plastered to her face. She was prettily humming something as she cracked an egg and let it fall into the pan. The albumen and yolk suddenly turned to blood and bile festering with maggots as Lawrence felt the world turn inside out. He could hear them pop and burst as they slithered into the pan. The cooktop was a mound of orange dirt with boil-covered hands, dismembered, holding utensils for their queen. She was waving her wooden spatula like a baton conducting an orchestra, the hole in the middle a white-hot searing orb melting everything it touched, into misshapen, twisted things. Gwendolyn turned her head and blew a kiss to him but Lawrence was completely lost somewhere else.

He tried to smile but felt it falter.

"Could you repeat the message that he asked you to write? I feel like I may have misheard you."

The noise from the phone suddenly faded to a hush. The entire room was devoid of sound. Lawrence could feel the hairs on back of his neck stand on end and a tightness spread out from his chest. There was this cold caress that bit mercilessly at his skin and seeped into his bones.

"I'm sorry, but are you on a private call, Lawrence?"

Gwendolyn wasn't in the kitchen cooking anymore. The kitchen was devoid of presence, with the light off and a pan resting in the drying rack next to the sink. Not even a carton of eggs was on the shiny countertop. It was an immaculate sight. Lawrence's heart moved into his throat.

He didn't need to turn around to know exactly where Gwendolyn was. He could feel her breath on the back of his neck. It was warm and sticky. A sense of anxiety gripped his throat. It felt like he was swallowing hot pins.

Lawrence pushed the button to end the call and slowly turned around. He half expected her to be holding a butcher's knife at his gullet. Nothing could've prepared him for what was actually waiting, though.

Gwendolyn, her beauty still preserved, wore a smile made of icy daggers. Her eyes! They looked like they were solid obsidian, black like the bottom of the deepest chasm in the ocean, save for the sparkle in her right eye, which only burned more intensely.

How long had she really been there? Did he imagine her standing in the kitchen only a minute ago making them breakfast?

Gwen's smile widened but not in way that was possible. For her face to contort in this manner she would've needed to rip the skin at the corners of her mouth but they were still there, perfect as they had always been.

"I truly wanted to save you, Lawrence. I really did. You have given me such pleasure—a sense of contentment I have never felt before. But *you* know now. *You know....*"

Her voice sounded like someone shaking a jar full of rusty nails. The detective backed up into the couch and lost his balance. He darted his head around but lost sight of her. He could feel his breathing intensify, skin quivering and vision blurring from his anxiety. She was standing in front of him only moments ago, her face an indescribable tapestry of beauty and wickedness. Lawrence looked to the kitchen again. Nothing....

A sound of a door slamming shut made him jump sideways.

He was suddenly pulled into her waiting embrace. Lawrence couldn't move. She titled his head back with ease and stared into his eyes. He could feel every impulse in his body under her very command. She let out a satisfied moan and whispered gently into his ear. The detective felt his anxiety melt away from her words. Her arms uncoiled from his body. Gwen started for the bedroom, not even giving the detective a second look. She removed his dress shirt and tossed it to the ground.

Lawrence finished getting dressed and walked to the door. He could feel nothing save for an absolute need to do something—something that just couldn't wait.

Gwendy entered back into the room with her robe on. She stared at her thrall for a moment before she asked, "Are you not going to stay any longer, Lawrence? I could make us some breakfast."

"No. Thank you, but no. I think I should leave. I've a lot to do, today. The cases are piling up on my desk and I need to clear some more."

Her smile reflected back in the glass of the door. It was purely malicious, but Lawrence didn't seem interested anymore. All the detective knew was that he needed to be somewhere else. As he shut the door he saw something new in Gwendolyn. It was horrific and inhuman but he just seemed to dismiss it. After all, he had so many things that needed to get done today. His cases at work wouldn't clear themselves.

*   *   *

Gwendolyn arrived at work exactly two minutes early. She hung up her newest lavender spring coat in the break room closet and then headed out to her station. She was dressed in a tight-fitting black dress that stopped at her ankles. The dress really accentuated her perfect figure, but it also breathed life into her tan heels with their blood-red bottoms. She adjusted the silk scarf at her neck, fine-tuned the angle of her nametag and sat down in her chair. She almost didn't hear her supervisor sidle up wearing a very grim expression deeply creased into her face.

Gwendolyn smiled. "My, don't *we* look super serious. Is everything alright?"

"Not really, Gwendy. I wanted you to hear this from me before it got around the watercooler. Rose committed suicide last night. She hung herself. The police said that she used her bedding as a makeshift noose and also left a rather disturbing note. Her family is just devastated. They can't even make sense of why she did what she did, you know?"

"I am so sorry to hear that. Rosario was a sweetheart. She never had a harsh word for anyone. Have they started talking about the funeral arrangements for her yet? She was Catholic so I assume they will want a prayer service or something similar with a clergyman there."

"I don't really know, Gwendy. You knew her best, I think. Would you mind reading something at her wake or funeral when it's been decided? I want a coworker there, who was close with her, to give her family a loving account of her time here at this branch office. It would help ease their pain knowing how much she was loved and respected at this place."

"Of course I will. Rose was a dear, dear friend. If it's not too inappropriate, may I ask what she penned in her suicide note? She was hardly lucid during my visit yesterday and she wasn't making much sense at all."

"I can only tell you what I heard, so it might *not* be genuine. She wrote something about a kind of monster or thing taking away the sun from her. She referred to it as 'The Scarlet Vesper' and then went on to say that she was taking her life because the Devil sent the Vesper to blot out the sun forever. I know…. It doesn't make any sense at all, right?"

Gwendy raised a hand to her forehead and shut her eyes for a moment. "So, so confusing. I never knew Rose to have such a flair for the dramatic."

Nor did I. The melodramatic air doesn't match our Rosario at all, right? Anyway, please keep this to yourself." Only the direct family and *I* know about this. I don't even know why I told you, Gwendy. Maybe you're just the trustworthy sort and you two were just so close."

"Whatever the reason, I'll not tell a single soul. You have my word."

"Thanks, doll."

After a reassuring squeeze on her shoulder, Gwendolyn spun around in her chair and opened her workstation to the public. With her supervisor off in a distance of shuffling shoes on carpets, muffled conversation and spoons clanking against coffee mugs, she felt safe enough to let her warming smile show.

*   *   *

Lawrence could feel the white-hot pins behind his eyes. He couldn't get her out of his head. Her voice echoed through his mind. Her very scent wafted through his nostrils and into his body. He could feel her breath on his neck and the sweetness of her laughter panged against his eardrums. The detective clasped at his head and fell to his knees. She was there with him. He could feel her piercing eyes on him. That sparkle was shining so brightly it made his skin glisten with sweat. Her sultry silhouette, born from the festering shadows in the room, coalesced before his very eyes. The detective's heart began to beat faster, the hammering of that bass drum only intensifying more and more as the shadow rose.

"What are you doing, Lawrence? Do you *still* think yourself worthy enough to kiss one of my feet? Or, how about my big toe? Do you think I should allow you to remove a single, solitary shoe and place your lips upon my big toe?"

The thought made him involuntarily salivate. To even hold Gwendy's foot in his hands would be like wrapping a silk scarf of ointment over hands cracked and bloodied from a deep freeze. His teeth began to itch. He clenched his jaw and rubbed his teeth together as if massaging them. The pain only intensified but it actually started to feel good. Her hand with its long perfect nails touched down upon his shoulder. The nails scratched against his shirt as they rose to his neck. Her breath was hot against the skin of his cheek and Lawrence trembled as she caressed his face. The nails were long and thin like daggers now.

"Are you pining for me yet, lover?"

"Yes... I... I do... I am! But why am I so afraid?"

"Do not be afraid. If you want me then just come to me. I am waiting for you."

Lawrence held out his hand, blindly, and felt for Gwen. She was there, wasn't she? He could feel her but she was so far out of reach. He opened his eyes and then immediately shut them. What he saw was burned into his eyes—like the fierce strike of a welder's rod. The flash burn was agonizing but he dare not open himself to the sight again.

"Lawrence... Lawrence?"

"Leave me alone!"

He forced himself to look and everything was dim. The detective was dripping with sweat. The receptionist, an older woman who had been working at the precinct for thirty years, was hovering about him.

"You don't look so hot, Larry. Maybe you should go home and get some rest, maybe see a doctor."

"I… I don't feel…. Yeah, maybe I will…."

The detective rose to his feet and immediately bolted for the door. Before reaching the door he shielded some of his face with his left hand. He could see her standing there, a shadow of maleficent force and ire. Lawrence's freedom was just outside of those double doors but not before he felt something pass through him and a severe, unearthly chill spread throughout his chest. The chill radiated outward until he collapsed to the ground outside and sobbed uncontrollably. In the background someone laughed in perfect unison with his cries.

*   *   *

Gwendolyn returned early from her first break. She'd been scribbling on some paper for about thirty minutes before she realized that work might be the best place to direct her energy. She wasn't coming up with anything that remotely sounded sympathetic enough for her dear departed friend and coworker, Rose. She pinned her nametag on and activated the light on the side of her window. An attractive gentleman with dark eyes and a perfectly pressed business suit handed her a hefty envelope. She met his eyes and smiled. The gentleman smiled back and touched his smooth chin. He seemed a little shy. Gwendolyn was not.

"Would like you to deposit the entire amount?" She clacked some keys on her computer's keyboard.

"Oh, um… no. Can you give me back two hundred dollars in small bills, please?"

"You did *not* fill out your deposit slip correctly. I'm sorry but you *will* need to redo it, sir."

"Oh. Um… sure."

The envelope of large bills was thrust back into the gentleman's hands.

"Next, please." Gwendolyn looked past her customer to the following person in line, smile never faltering.

The teller was very efficient at her job. Sometimes the only way to let someone have what they wanted was to make them work for it. If filling out another slip and going to the back of the line was the only way to teach someone, Gwendolyn O'Hara was a harsh but firm advocate. The man didn't protest. He hung his head in shame and did as instructed. The abnormally long line today was a perfect teaching tool to ensure that he'd certainly learn a valuable lesson in the end.

*   *   *

The detective lay back in the small, narrow bed. The fluorescent lights were uncomfortably bright. He rolled to his left, the side where his heart monitor was holding a steady beat. He didn't remember going to a hospital, but nevertheless he was there. A man wearing a long white lab coat, blue gloves and maroon scrubs approached holding a few forms clamped to a clipboard.

"Why am I here?" The haziness was ever present in Lawrence's guttural rumblings.

"You were brought in, via ambulance, after you collapsed earlier this afternoon. Apparently, you collapsed directly outside the doors of the police station. The call was placed by a passerby who asked to remain anonymous."

"Oh…. What can ya tell me, Doc?"

"Well, you appear to be in fine health. Your blood tests all came back good, save for some higher-than-normal cholesterol readings. Your blood pressure has been monitored the entire time you've been here. That's also looking good too. Do you remember anything unusual before losing consciousness?"

"Not really, no."

"Well, your heartrate was slightly elevated initially and your body temperature was a little low. Have you ever suffered from a panic attack? The symptoms aren't far off and some people have lost consciousness from them."

"I've *never* had a panic attack in my life. I've seen some heinous shit being on the force and still never even felt faint from it."

"Easy, Detective. I'm only asking because it's a logical conclusion. Medicine isn't always an exact science."

"Sorry. No. I've never had a panic attack before."

"Alright. I can recommend you to have a stress test done. I see nothing wrong with your heart but you can never be too careful. I can set that up through your primary if you like."

"Okay. Thanks, Doc."

"You can be discharged at any time, but I'm going to write you a script for some Ambien. It should help you sleep. Maybe a good night's rest will have you back to chasing down perps in no time."

"Alright. Yeah, maybe. Truthfully, I'd rather just pour myself a bourbon and Coke and watch the game."

"Well, with this kind of medication you might want to stay away from alcohol. I'll write you that script and get your discharge papers ready."

Lawrence sat up and tried to clear his head. He could still smell her skin, the taste of her lips lingering inside of his mouth. She was there with him. The detective could feel his body trembling. Gwendolyn was somewhere behind his eyes, and she was digging mercilessly into his brain. He cupped his hands and covered his face with them. It was all he could do not to break down into tears. The blips on the heart monitor started to quicken. Lawrence suddenly felt like all his blood rushed to his head. He eased back down and looked up towards the ceiling. There was a sparkle of light from the overhead fluorescents. It was so bright that it made him wince. The light started to fade a little as a shadow crossed over his field of vision. The monitor started to beep louder and more frequent as the shadow dragged across his face.

"What's wrong, Lawrence? Not happy to see me? I came here as soon as I could."

Her hiss was strident and caused the detective to cover his ears. His heart monitor started making an equally harsh but constant shriek. He closed his eyes just as her new face came into focus. The shadow lingered on him as he felt her caress the skin of his neck. He trembled and waved about at the air.

"Mr. Stowell. Are you alright?"

Lawrence opened his eyes and saw the doctor with his paperwork in one hand and a green pad in the other. He put down the objects and started shining his penlight into Lawrence's eyes.

"This is odd. Your eyes are completely dilated, but they weren't moments ago. I've never seen anything like it."

Lawrence frantically looked around but the apparition of Gwendolyn was no longer there with him. He breathed deeply as the doctor took his vitals again.

"Doc, where's my cellphone?"

"Probably in the plastic bag your things were placed in on the table there."

"Can you get it for me, please? I need to make a call."

*   *   *

Gwendolyn listened to her voicemail. This was the third message she'd received today where the caller didn't say anything. They just let the space in her inbox fill up with silence. She would've settled for at least some heavy breathing or inappropriate noises. She placed her phone on the coffee table and sat back down on the couch. She closed her eyes for a moment. She remembered the feeling of Lawrence caressing her body on this very couch, his hands were gentle, though a little cold, but felt so nice against her warm, smooth skin. She wanted to pick up her phone and call him but decided that she would wait for him to make the next move. Gwen turned on her television and scrolled through the romantic comedies waiting to be watched. She picked one at random and hugged a pillow close to her chest. Gwen's smile was that of a woman who was truly lonely. She desired attention and affection but could never feel those things long enough. It would be torture for some women, but she was cut from a different cloth. She knew that as long as she drew breath there would always be a man out there willing to give her what she wanted, even for a short time.

*   *   *

The voice inside Lawrence's head was piercing. He could feel her dragging a knife across his spine and up to his skull. The detective curled up into a ball, on the floor, and started to sob ever so gently. A shape moved in the corner of the room. The fingernails were long, thin daggers scraping against the wall. There was a brilliant light beaming from the right side of where its face should be. Lawrence shivered. The creature bent low and ran a knife's edge against his cheek. There was a sardonic smile that couldn't be described as anything but grotesque. No human could contort their face in this manner. Each tear was collected by the creature. It raised one to its lips and a low hiss expelled from where its mouth should have been. Lawrence craned his head around and spotted his gun. He'd taken it off and placed it on his kitchen table. He'd sworn that's where he put it, but there it was now on the floor.

A hand made from midnight's sky clasped the gun and placed it into his shaky hand. He could hear her voice again.

"My white knight. Are you feeling well? You went to the hospital today. I honestly cannot help but think things are not going to be okay for you."

"Leave me the fuck alone!"

Her sweet laughter filled the room.

"Lawrence. Is that any way to talk to a lady? I am concerned about your wellbeing. Are you so cavalier that you cannot see that?"

Lawrence pulled himself up onto his hands and knees. Sweat dripped from his forehead and his bloodshot eyes searched around for anything that could calm his anxiety.

"I... I know you killed them. I don't know how you did it, but I know you did. And you've killed before too. This isn't new for you."

"Killed? I have not *killed* anyone. Perhaps you are just grasping at straws to explain these horrific tragedies. Maybe these incidents have started to unravel your resolve."

"I think not. You're a god-damned murderer, Gwendolyn. I don't know how you're doing it but... there's just no other way of explaining it. It's you. It's always been you! It's like I've felt you from the beginning, the day we first met, and now you're so deep inside that I can't cut you out of me without..."

The creature put a clawed hand into the detective's lung. It slipped in without resistance. Lawrence gasped. He began wheezing and banging at the ground. There was a pain like someone twisting the lung clockwise inside his body. He flopped against the floor. The creature was face-to-face with him now. Where there should have been eyes was just a deep, endless void of nothingness. However, if you stared just long enough you could see a faint, sparkling star in the right eye. It was reaching out from behind that nothingness.

Lawrence coughed, some blood spilling out onto the floor in front of him. "Why is there a twinkle in your right eye? Why can't I look away? What are you?!"

The creature began to smile again. The coughing intensified right before Lawrence lost consciousness.

*   *   *

Gwendolyn woke up. She had inadvertently fallen asleep on the couch. She never saw the end of the movie. Perhaps there was an abrupt twist where the man turned out to be a psycho killer or the woman a passionate arsonist. Perhaps they died in each other's arms during the climax, their desire for one another setting them ablaze to be nothing but ash blended together forever. Was it their fate to be together forever this way? Still groggy, Gwen shook the morbidity from her mind and got up. It was 3 in the morning. Gwendolyn stretched her arms up over her head. She moved her body around to work out the kinks. Something felt off. She looked over to her phone. It was flashing as if someone had called her. She smiled. Seizing the phone from the coffee table she went through her missed calls. It was a call from Lawrence. He had called at 1:00 A.M., but he never left a message. She pouted a little and placed her phone back on the table. Gwendolyn sat back on the couch and picked at some popcorn pieces at the bottom of a large bowl. Her beautiful red locks cascaded around her like a waterfall of pure flame. Her eyes were distant but her mind was very much in the moment. Behind her, in the light of the television's glow, a shadow warped around the room. It was nothing short of sinister as it stopped behind Gwendolyn and remained perfectly still.

*   *   *

The medics wheeled the stretcher out of the house, which was filled with a silence so deafening it threatened to split the seams of the world. Two detectives, one veteran and the other still green, conferred in a small corner of the room while the forensics team finished up their diligent work. Blood was catalogued and pictures taken of a scene so gruesome that no one dared to speak about it. There was a scrawling in the floor, crimson washed and very deliberate. The words were ominous, a warning from the departed to anyone who'd listen.

"She is pure evil. Don't trust her eyes."

There were twelve photos taken of this warning. Some of it was scratched into the floor with a knife blade that broke during the process. Where the knife had failed a set of fingernails wouldn't. They had exhausted themselves. Shattered slivers were all over the floor scattered around the message. A light dusting of nail shavings showed that this message was so important to the deceased that they'd risked all the keratin possible to deliver it.

"Are you guys finished up here?" the older detective called into the room.

"Yeah. We're just taking a few last samples before we wrap up. I mean, it's not like we can't piece together what happened here."

"What was the time of death? Give me a rough estimate."

"With all we know I'd say it was between 1 and 3 A.M."

The older detective looked to be ruminating over the information. The younger one spoke up.

"Is there a problem with the time?"

"Nah, nothing like that, kid. I was just thinking. My grandmother used to believe that when we were awakened from a sound sleep at around 3 A.M. it wasn't a good omen. Do you know the significance of that time in the Bible?"

"No. I'm not religious, sir."

"Well, it's like this…. Christ was said to have died at around 3:00 A.M. The things that occur at this time in our era are to be considered malicious acts to mock that time, namely by demons."

"Do you actually believe in that stuff?"

"My grandmother sure did. She once told me that she suddenly woke up at 3:30 A.M. and followed the sound of a strange growling throughout the house. She found its origin in the room I used to stay in. There was something intently watching me sleep. It was large and made of pure darkness, perched on the headboard of my bed with ease. Nana could've sworn that she saw a terrible smile, horns protruding from the skull and coal-black eyes. The creature wanted to be inside my body. It was the last time I ever stayed in that house. My grandmother died that very night. It was a heart attack. She was only 62 years old."

"Huh? Died that night? How did you know about all this then? If she died how could she have told you?"

"Good detective skills, kid. She came to me in a dream four days later. I wrote it off as one of those dreams you have when you really miss someone. But when we went back to clear out her home I felt this heavy weight on me. It was so hard to breathe. I even swore I heard creepy sounds coming from the room that used to be mine. I tell ya… I've never been so freaked out in my life."

"Did you ever go back to that house again?"

"Once more when I was in my thirties so I could see it turned into a pile of rubble. Let's get back to the station so we can file the reports. This case looks pretty clear cut, wouldn't you agree?"

*   *   *

Lawrence sighed as he tried to get his paperwork finalized for a recently closed case. He kept telling himself that whatever he thought he was feeling wasn't real, but the feelings of dread and emptiness were staying with him. The homicide department was working another apparent suicide case on the West End of town that was pretty gruesome. Lawrence opted out due to the way he'd been feeling lately. The detective just couldn't witness another bizarre bloodbath involving a man right now and remain even keeled.

Lawrence got up and started down the hall. He spied a coffee cart in the hallway and threw down a few dollars.

"The usual, Larry?"

The voice belonged to the old woman who always pushed this cart around the precinct at this time of day. Her husband was shot and killed in the line of duty, and she made it a habit of always coming into the station at least three days a week to deliver a very strong cup of coffee and home-made heavenly donuts to all the cops she'd meet.

"Yeah. I'll have a plain cruller too if you've got one."

"I only have chocolate ones left."

"That'll be fine. Honestly, Lucile would smash the Ten Commandments over my head, but I'm in a cruller kind of mood."

"Your late wife was a saint, Larry, but I wouldn't ever want to be on her bad side."

"Well, I won't tell her if you don't."

The two exchanged a laugh. It was the most genuine feeling Lawrence had had in the last few days.

He took his coffee and donut back to his office. He rushed to his desk and looked down at his paperwork. There was a drawing done on the page he'd been working on. Slamming the cup down, Lawrence fell into the seat and tried to make sense of the scene. He knew his writing anywhere and this was definitely it, but had no recollection of drawing on his forms.

The sloppy sketch was of a girl in a swing. She had large black circular eyes and messy hair. Her arms and legs were basically sticks poking out of a dress with patterns of dots on it. Lawrence imagined that the dress was green and that the dots were gold flecks. She was being pushed by something inhuman looking behind the swing. As she was soaring at a great height in the air, a creature waited for her on the ground below. It was blackened hastily with horns and terrible claws for hands and feet. The girl had a look on her face that did not speak of enjoyment. She was high in air and away from the demon's reach but she'd eventually have to come back down, thanks to gravity, and right into its waiting arms.

What did this mean?

He felt that breath, hot again against his cheek, and something like a hand caress his chest. He backed up suddenly, fear etching heavy lines into his pale face. He'd run out of space and slammed against the wall behind him.

"You have only but a few days before the madness takes hold. You have done so well to stave it off, Lawrence, but it will only get worse. You will eventually succumb like all the others. And trust me, there have been many, many others."

"You've been killing a long time, Gwendolyn. At first I figured you for a black widow but that just seems too complicated. So, why then? What's the point to it all?"

"Death's sweet kiss will bring you much salvation, my white knight. However, you still have but one chance. You see, it has to be a man who does it. It cannot be anyone but a man who breaks the cycle. *We* have been waiting for so long…."

"I don't understand what you're on about. Has to be a man who does what?"

A sharp screeching filled the detective's mind. It was like thousands of sharp nails on a hundred dusty old chalkboards. He fell to his knees and saw the shadows in the room shift violently. He gasped as he saw the creature take form again. This was its most horrifying incarnation yet. Lawrence screamed with all he could muster.

The sound inside Lawrence's office was eaten up by the malevolent spirit. However, if anyone walked by, all they saw was a man hard at work at his desk.

*   *   *

The room booked for the wake was very spacious. There were a lot of people who came to pay their respects to the Alma family. Their eldest daughter was taken too soon. Gwendolyn milled about the crowd and listened to the people talk about Rosario in the most compassionate of ways. She envied their word choices. They were so eloquent. Her speech felt paltry in comparison.

She rounded a circle of friends, who all spoke about Rose as if they were in high school getting ready to sign her yearbook. She spied her supervisor out of the corner of her eye, who waved Gwendy over to her position.

"How'd that eulogy work out? You think that it's done?"

"Oh. Well, I was able to spin some words but I'm not quite sure they are perfect."

"It's okay. You can read whatever you have there. I'm sure it'll be fine."

"Um… I think I would feel more comfortable if someone else read these out loud. I'm not bashful, per se, but I honestly don't know her family. It would feel a little awkward for me up on that podium. Everyone else seems to have such a deep connection to Rose and I only knew her from my time at the bank."

Her smile was the sun itself. She was so full of splendor and refinement.

"It's okay. I'll read it for you. I can always add at the end of the eulogy that you were the only hand in its creation. It's not like they're going to shine a spotlight on you afterwards."

"That's so thoughtful. Thank you for taking the pressure off of me."

Gwendolyn's supervisor grabbed a folded piece of paper from Gwendy and took the podium. She was clad in a lovely charcoal dress with a black cardigan over it. She unfurled the paper in her hands and cleared her throat.

"'Rose was a wonderful woman who was taken before her time. She was many things to us all. However, the one thing that she was *most* is something that not many people will want to hear. Rose was a jealous wretch of a woman who lived in fear of the unknown.'"

A hush fell over the crowd. Rose's family looked on in sudden shock as a woman they didn't know read aloud words that should never have been said to the grieving.

Maybe I should've edited that part? Gwendolyn mused as her boss cleared her throat and turned a shade of crimson that few people ever do.

Nevertheless, her boss continued to read from that folded paper with great poise.

"'However, despite her being a frightened little mouse, I know that I truly envied her for having found her one true love early in life. Her late husband, Esteban, no longer needs to wait because Rose most certainly has gone to him. He will hold her in his arms, shrouded by the infinitesimal cloudscape of the Heavens and they will be eternally together with the Lord. I know that she will always be loved by him there until the rest of their families reunite with them both. Even if Rose had nothing left in life, she certainly had everything waiting for her after it.'"

Gwendolyn suddenly felt a small tug at her heartstrings. Was this it for her? Was she eternally damned to feel alone even in a crowded room? Had a lowly church mouse found the secret to eternal happiness where she'd always seemed to fall off the top rung of the ladder time and again?

She wiped her eyes with a tissue and stood. She wanted to wail and beat her fists against the casket. She wanted to wake Rose from her eternal slumber and beg her to show her how to find that one person who could make all others feel insignificant. Tawdry in comparison were the rich, powerful men who pined for her. Suddenly her heart truly ached for Lawrence.

All eyes in the room centered on Gwendolyn. Wasn't it just like her? She was stealing all the attention and pity from a room full of mourning strangers. Her downcast eyes were the eyes of the truly lonely.

Rose's father stood up. His face was a stoic iron mask. He put a hand on Gwendolyn's shoulder to ease her sadness, but the woman hardly felt it. She simply walked on by and headed for the exit. Everyone watched as the ravishing redhaired woman who wept for the loss of her dear, departed friend paid her fitting tribute.

*　　*　　*

Lawrence slammed the door to the apartment shut. With a large, angry swipe he hurled the framed pictures from the sideboard. They crashed to floor in a cacophony of shattering glass. The silent epitaphs of a once happy life lay forgotten as Lawrence began moving the heavy table in front of his entry door. He breathed heavily and looked down at his cellphone. He opened the contacts list, finger violently shaking over Gwendolyn's number. Lawrence tossed the phone across the room and fell to his knees. It was all becoming too much for him to bear. He could feel her siphoning his very existence. Her essence was choking him with every moment that passed. He was in the final stages of her seductions.

"Lawrence. I'm so glad that you came home. I was beginning to think that you didn't want to have anything to do with me anymore."

The meadowlark sweetness was unmistakable. Lawrence whipped around. There *she* was. She was standing right behind him. She was beautiful, vibrant and exquisite, dressed in a long black dress with a slit up the right leg. Her hair was arranged in a high ponytail cascading over her left shoulder. She held her hands out in front of her body clasping them together, standing straight and tall. Lawrence could feel tears and the sudden urge to vomit all at once.

"How… how did you get in here?" he stammered.

"You left the back entrance ajar. I'm not sure what pushing that piece of furniture in front of your main entrance will do if you cannot remember how to bar the rear one."

That sparkle crackled for a moment before settling along with her sweet smile.

"What are you? What the fuck are you!?!"

"*Me?* Why, I'm just a woman who wants to fall in love. Is that so wrong? I started to worry for you when you hadn't called me. I thought we had a good time the other night. Anyway, I just returned from a wake and I couldn't bear to be without you for another moment."

"What? Are you fucked in the head or something?"

"Not to my knowledge. Why do you ask?" Her eyes instantly looked sullen.

"You've been killing them all. They meet you and then they fall hopelessly in love with you. But it doesn't stop there. You're like a virus taking hold of your victims. You stay in their heads and eventually you drive them to off themselves."

"I guess I should tell you the truth, then. It seems you know most of it already, but not everything. Of all the men I've been with, I want to explain myself to you more than anyone else. The true and utter loneliness—the heart beating inside of my breast cannot bear it anymore."

Lawrence grabbed his sidearm and held it out towards Gwendolyn. He started breathing heavier.

Gwendolyn spread her arms open in a gesture of trust. "You see, I was born a long time ago. About ninety years, to be exact. I've had to change my name and social security numbers a couple of times but nothing too drastic. I've always picked missing persons, cold cases that never get resolved. Maybe, in a way, I relate to those people the most."

"So, you're not Gwendolyn O'Hara, then?"

"No. I've only been her for about ten years now."

Lawrence backed up a little but kept the gun trained on Gwendolyn.

"Anyway, every story has a beginning. Let me avail you mine. My mother became pregnant with twins—me and my sister Hannah. My mother was a breathtaking beauty—a woman with red hair the color of a wildfire and amazing blue eyes. Anyway, she fell down the stairs and was rushed to the hospital at about eight months pregnant. My father, who was a lecherous hump and a belligerent alcoholic, pushed her. He had no use for God because in his mind he was the only higher power. Be that as it may, he prayed that night that his children would be spared. However, he did not pray to God."

Gwendolyn reached into her purse and produced a photograph. It looked quite old and faded. She bent slightly and tossed it across the floor to Lawrence, who crouched to retrieve it.

The photo was of a very young girl who looked like Gwendolyn, only a lot smaller, standing next to an imposing beast of a man with tattoos on his forearms and short hair. He had a deep scar on his left cheek and because of that crease, his smile looked forced. Lawrence focused his gaze on the man's elbow tat of a spiraling spider's web. The significance wasn't lost on him.

"My mother lost Hannah that night. Have you ever heard of vanishing twin syndrome?"

Lawrence just shook his head.

"It's when one twin devours the other, absorbing the fetal tissue like they were never there at all. Hannah is a part of me, since that day, and always has been."

"What does this have to do with the suicides?"

"I'm getting to that part, Lawrence. Remember when I told you that my father beseeched a higher power? He did so that his bloodline would continue on, but he needed a soul to make the transaction. The soul he offered wasn't his own. He was too much in love with himself for that. So, he offered my mother's soul as the bargaining chip. My mother seemingly died giving birth to me and I inherited more than just what I took from my sister. I was given terrible power. *We* were given power."

Gwendolyn's eyes turned inky black, pure sheening obsidian as her shadow walked away from the wall the stood next to her. The shape began to exhibit traits—similar to Gwendy but very much sharper and more malicious.

"This demon in me has been here for a long time, Lawrence. Hannah, or what remains of her, feeds off of strong sexual desires. I guess you could say that I am partially a succubus, for lack of a better term. When my eyes lock to yours and you first notice the sparkle hiding within the green that is the moment you are mine, or shall I say ours. Your mind begins a dance that only ends with you succumbing to the madness, but you know this already. I wanted things to be different with you. I thought you were the one but I can see how sadly mistaken I have been. She's already destroyed your mind, hasn't she?"

Hannah's alien obsidian gaze poured over the detective. He kept backing up as she closed the gap between them. She certainly wasn't human, but the detective didn't believe in Hell and its servants… or so he thought.

"Gwendy? Don't you want to stop doing this? I can help you put an end to all of it for good. You can have a normal life. Please, just tell Hannah to back off so we can figure this all out."

"Why would *we* want to stop?"

A terrible hiss escaped her perfect lips, the Cupid's bow taught with humor. Hannah's fingernails seemed to lengthen in accord with Gwendolyn's shift in mood. She looked like she was going to strike Lawrence down right where he stood. Gwendolyn started to move forward, matching stride with her shadow sibling.

"You said I still had a chance. I believe that you want to be free of this. I mean, why share any of this with me otherwise?"

She shifted her neck to the side, which seemed to have elongated a few inches. Her teeth appeared jagged and cruel. The detective continued to put as much distance between them as the small space would allow. Eventually he'd run out of room.

"Hannah. Why don't we stop? I told you before that I thought he was different. I loved being with him the other night. You did too. Can we be happy, like Rose?"

"No, we must feed to stay vibrant. Who are you to deny me this meal? After all, we're only in this predicament because of you and our wretched father, aren't we?"

"Lawrence, no other man has touched my heart like you. I truly wanted you to be the one."

Lawrence eased the gun down. "That's good, Gwendy. That's very good. Now, please tell Hannah to go back now. She's obviously agitated and I'm not sure we can trust her."

A shriek from Hannah brought the gun back up and almost caused Lawrence to fire.

"Don't listen to him, Gwendolyn! He's just trying to trick you into calling me back inside and then he'll put a bullet in your brain. He wants to end you. Can't you see his deception? Remember what our father tried to do to us. Remember what he did to our mother? They are all the same. They are all just cattle!"

"Is that what you really want, Gwendolyn?" Lawrence spat his question so fast so that Hannah could not interrupt. He knew that if he kept Gwen talking that Hannah would have less of a hold on her. This was the same tactic that he'd used on a jumper in the past.

"My father wanted to destroy us when he figured out what we truly were. Our mother died giving birth to my shell. I equally died in the same moment as my mother's last breath. However, something else was given life in that moment—something more. I have become the person you see before you bursting with a sparkle of life tainted within the blackness of death. I was born from she who'd had died. My father witnessed firsthand what the twinkle in my eye could do so he tried to poison me along with himself to end us both. He did not count on Hannah figuring out his plan. We saw it together in his thoughts—saw what he wanted to do. We made it work to our advantage and ended up with relatives and then bounced from countless foster homes like so much garbage. We'd never been as lonely as those days."

Lawrence could see the sadness in Gwendolyn's eyes. That very pain was palpable and threatened to invade his own emotional state. He could only gather that her ability to control the desires of the mind was causing this effect on him. Whether it was Hannah's doing or not, he was trapped in a web and that black widow begged to be satiated.

"It's never going to end, is it? I cannot see any scenario where I can live happily for the rest of my days."

Gwendolyn idly ran her hand over the floor behind her. She felt something cold and solid, like a knife's edge. She instantly grasped hold of it.

"Please. Gwendolyn. Put down that hunk of glass. We were all talking. You were saying something about your father, remember?"

"Thank you, Lawrence. I'll always love you most of all. Of all the men I met, I'm glad I revealed to you the real me."

"Gwendolyn! My wife, Lucile, died from—"

She twirled the shard around and forced the edge into her eye. It wasn't just any eye. It was the one where Hannah lived. The alien but beautiful twinkle that had become an all-consuming curse. The popping sound of the glass scoring Gwendy's eye socket was deafening. Hannah screamed along with her twin and, as swift as the wind, buried one of her clawed hands into the wall next to Lawrence's face. Part of the wall broke free and turned into a violent storm of ashes. Lawrence was now face to face with the creature and the safety was off. Her smile was just as malicious as ever and her thin, diabolical fingernails steadily clanked against one another – hungry for fresh blood.

Lawrence took aim but faltered. He felt nothing but pity and heartfelt sorrow.

Hannah wheezed her hatred. "It was always going to be this way. You accepted this fate the moment you dared to gaze into our eyes."

Gwendolyn collapsed to the floor, a warm inky blackness pouring down her face. Hannah shrieked but remained strong. She was more than just a part of Gwendolyn's alien eye. She truly was a curse—a demonic thing born from rage and uninhibited lusts. She would never stop. She would never tire and she'd only grow hungrier as time went on.

The thought of being devoured by Hannah made Lawrence sick to his stomach. His heart pounded furiously within his chest. He could see Hannah's true incarnation now and it scared him more than anything in this world. The outer shell of the beautiful woman, Gwendolyn, was gone and there was only the apparition, the demon who needed only to devour. The thought was more terrifying than anything Lawrence could imagine.

A single tear streaked his left cheek. Lawrence raised the gun and curled it back into his own mouth. A single bang and a spray of brain and blood washed the wall behind him. Whatever Lawrence saw before his end was just too much to bear. A keening laughter filled the room. It was so unsettling that even Lawrence's dead body shuddered.

*   *   *

The street was lined with bustling bodies and flashing lights. Someone had called in a complaint that they'd thought that they'd heard a gun go off and then there was a loud wailing. As the police wheeled a single body out of the apartment, they all solemnly acknowledged that this was one of their own. A man arrived on the scene with a grey duster and thick boots. He waded through the crowd of people like wind traveling effortlessly through the trees. He stepped into a puddle of rainwater and his reflection could only be described as grim. He'd seen enough of these suicides lately to last a lifetime.

He approached the front door, which was open, though most of the porch was closed off with police tape. He handed his badge to the officer there and the woman nodded her assent for him to go on inside.

"What can you tell me about the deceased?"

She looked to the ground for a moment before speaking. "His name was Lawrence Stowell. He was a good cop. I just can't believe he'd offed himself. They found some photos of him and his late wife on the floor, glass everywhere. Maybe the reason for what happened."

"This job can get to you, kid. Do yourself a favor and find a really immersive hobby."

The detective placed a hand on her shoulder and moved inside the apartment. There was one body and one tragic tale. Another man committed suicide tonight and that's all that anyone really needed to hear.

*   *   *

She sat at her vanity mirror fixing her makeup. She only used the necessary lipliner and mascara to accentuate her already comely facial features. Her strawberry-red hair fell like a waterfall over her shoulders. She brushed her front locks behind her ears so that her neck and bare shoulders would be more prominent—tempting. The doorbell rang, which caused a full impish smile to appear over her lips.

She walked to the door and opened it without hesitation. There was a gentleman standing before her with a large bouquet of flowers and a heart-shaped box of candy. He was tall, with short black hair and baby-blue eyes.

Gwendolyn kept her gleeful smile and gestured for the man to enter. He was captivated by her short purple dress.

"You look amazing, Gwendy. Here. These are for you."

"They're just perfect. I'll put the flowers in some water. Make yourself comfortable. I'll be but a few minutes."

The man sat in the reclining chair close to the television. He couldn't take his eyes off his date, who seemed to move with grace so impressive it was almost as if she were levitating rather than walking. She finished arranging the flowers in their vase and reappeared back in the room.

"I'm finished getting ready. Shall we go?"

"Yes."

Their eyes met for a quick instant.

"Wow." His breath caught.

"What is it?"

"That sparkle in your eye…. It's just so unusual."

"Oh, that? I have taken to calling it a twinkle—like how a star twinkles in the sky. And yes, it appears to be very unusual. At least, everyone seems to think so."

"I really like it. However did you get it?"

It always came back to this.

Gwendolyn ran her tongue absently over her teeth.

"Well, it really is *quite* the story, but I promise to tell you everything in good time."

Gwendolyn and her date left the apartment. He just couldn't help it but his gaze seemed to always go back to that majestic twinkle held just inside of her right eye.